MADNESS AT THE MANOR

SHELLY WOTA

Order this book online at www.trafford.com
or email orders@trafford.com

Most Trafford titles are also available at major online book retailers.

Print information available on the last page.

ISBN: 978-1-6987-0200-1 (sc)
ISBN: 978-1-6987-0201-8 (e)

Trafford rev. 06/19/2020

www.trafford.com
North America & international
toll-free: 1 888 232 4444 (USA & Canada)
fax: 812 355 4082

I would like to dedicate this book to my mom
Anne Caliguire (Peltier)

I would like to thank Chester and Carlo for
all their input, much appreciated

PART 1

CHAPTER 1

It had been three months since Gina and Arthur went to London, where they had registered for classes at Croydon College, which are for two-years. Gina will major in the Arts and minor in Estate Management. Arthur will major in Botany and also minor in Estate Management. Since Gina was from the country and being a shy person, she felt a bit overwhelmed at first. There were so many students (currently there are about 3000), and the college was so big that after getting lost a few times, she had made herself a map of where her dorm was as well as the cafeteria and her classrooms. The college was a four-story brick building formed into a square, with a quad in the center. There were sitting areas as well as tiny shrubs. With the work he did at the manor, Arthur was able to identify some of the shrubs as glossy abelia and tree purslane. The front of the college has ivy creeping up the walls, which looks very picturesque when the leaves change in the autumn, as well as some Japanese snowball shrubs. Across the street is a park with a large pond where there were ducks and geese, among other birds. The open space reminds Gina of home. She promised herself that she would go there for quiet times where she would not be able to hear the London traffic.

Gina now feels confident in finding her way around, but she sometimes walked with students who were in her same classes. It was also a comfort to her when she saw Arthur around campus.

She had also been seeing quite a lot of Jr., who has taken it upon himself to be her private tour guide. He took her to the usual tourist attractions, which Gina thoroughly enjoyed. She had found Windsor Castle and the Tower of London quite immense edifices, even though she knew the history behind them. She had rarely been away from home and had only been to London on one or two occasions. One of her favorite tourist attractions was Big Ben. When the clock first rang, it scared her, and Jr. had to laugh. Afterward, she smiled at herself. She couldn't wait to write to her parents. During one of their excursions, Jr. confided in her that since he had taken over for his father, it was not as bad as he thought it would be. He stated that he could pick and choose his clients and delegate the rest to other staff. Gina confided in him that she did get homesick, and knowing that Arthur was not too far away was a comfort, plus it helps that Arthur picks her up when they take the bus home for weekends. And, once or twice, Jr. had driven them home.

In two weeks it would be Christmas break, and Gina was excited about the ten days she will be home. After about two trips to see Big Ben, she drew it from memory in her art class and would give it to her parents as a Christmas gift. But, for now, she was very busy with her studies. Mid-term exams are coming up, and she was studying hard, which allowed her only time for short outings with Jr.

Arthur was also enjoying his classes. He had a perfect reason to take botany classes now that he would be co-owner of the manor. He was not as awed as Gina was since his grandmother and mother lived in London, so he had been there before. His mother had left Cockernhoe shortly after DS Dunes questioned the villagers. When her husband, Malcolm, left to make his fortune in Ireland, Maggie had their cottage boarded up for when Arthur finished school and decided where he would like to live. He would travel home to Cockernhoe with Gina to spend part of the Christmas break at the manor but will return to London a few days earlier to spend some time with his mother and grandmother.

Jr. had come to realize that Arthur is a nice guy and found him likable now that they are no longer in competition for Gina's affections. He planned to go to France to spend the Christmas holidays with his parents.

CHAPTER 2

Meanwhile, back at the manor, Mrs. Locke was driving Mr. Locke to distraction with preparations for Gina and Arthur's visit. Her husband was surprised at how she seemed to be everywhere at once, considering her size. She certainly was not the same woman he fell in love with and married twenty-five years ago. He loved to see her light brown hair fall out of its bun and watch the sparkle of her hazel eyes as she tried to rearrange it. She wanted to clean everything and had to hire some of the village girls to help. Mr. Locke tried to stay out of her way and was keeping himself busy tidying the grounds. He teased his wife that she needn't cook so muChapter He reminded her that Gina had only been gone for three months, and had been home each weekend, but she had decided to stay in London for the last two weekends before Christmas break to concentrate solely on the mid-term exams. Mrs. Locke realized that after the holidays, Gina wouldn't be coming home every weekend; she will needed to spend more time with her studies. Mrs. Locke wanted to have some mother/daughter time during the holidays, so she decided to save some of the decorating for when Gina came home. They usually didn't put up any decorations, but Mrs. Locke felt it was time for the manor to be alive and again, like in the old days. With Christmas approaching and with Gina and Arthur soon to be the new owners, she would like to set a new precedent hoping Gina and Arthur will approve of her ideas.

She also wanted to prepare a celebratory tea for DS Dunes and his new wife. After the trial, DS Dunes married his fiancée Professor Liz Bloom. They are planning to stop at the manor on the way to their honeymoon destination.

The day Mrs. Locke had been awaiting with anticipation had arrived. One would think that Gina and Arthur had been away for longer than three months, considering all the preparations Mrs. Locke performed. They all had so much to say that they all started talking at the same time. Mr. Locke had to take control and suggested they go in for tea and chat. While the tea was brewing, Arthur told them of some of his new ideas he had for the manor. Mr. Locke thought they had some merit, so he and Arthur would go out later and look at the areas that Arthur had in mind to either change or upgrade. Meanwhile, Gina had so much she wanted to tell her mom that they finished their tea in a hurry so they could talk while the men were outside.

Mrs. Locke first took Gina out to look at the garden. She told her that the girl from the village had been a great help with expanding it and after spring planting, and during the time Gina is in London, then they would consider hiring her full time. They will have some fresh vegetables for their Christmas dinner since they have some growing in the greenhouse. Back in the manor as they walked around the house, Gina told her mother about some of the "dates" she had with Jr. She asked her mom if she should consider them dates because he wanted to show her around London, or does she think he is just polite? "Did he hold your hand at any time?" asked her mom. "Not really, but I wanted to hold his," admitted Gina. "Do you think that would be too forward of me if I did?" she asked her mom. "I don't think so," replied her mom.

"It's good news about DS Dunes getting married, don't you think?" mentioned Gina. "It's hard to imagine that serious man who was here questioning everyone is married. What do you have planned for tea?" she asked. "Nothing too extravagant since I don't know either of their preference," answered her mom.

"DS Dunes said they wouldn't be able to stay for more than a couple of hours. I think I hear them arriving now. How do I look?" Mrs. Locke asked Gina. "You look, great mom, don't worry, he won't arrest you for having flour on your face," giggled Gina as Mrs. Locke quickly wiped her face. Mr. Locke and Arthur came into the kitchen, followed by DS Dunes and his wife. "They're here," he announced to Mrs. Locke. "Oh, Mr. Locke, why did you bring our guests in by the kitchen?" reprimanded Mrs. Locke. "This is just fine, Mrs. Locke, no need to put the red carpet out for us," added DS Dunes. "Welcome, Mr. & Mrs. Dunes." stammered Mrs. Locke. "Please call me Bill, and this is my beautiful bride, Liz," continued DS Dunes. "It's so nice to meet you, and I hope the drive from London was pleasant," stated Mrs. Locke, "and please call me Margaret, and this is my husband, Morris, and our daughter, Gina, and her friend, Arthur," continued Mrs. Locke. "Please come into the dining room; lunch is ready," she announced. "This looks like a feast," commented Bill. "You didn't have to go to so much trouble on our account, but thank you so much." "What are your travel plans?" asked Morris. "First, we will go to Dover for a few days then catch the ferry to France. We are planning to travel around France for about ten days, then head back home. Work, you know — no rest for the wicked." added Bill.

"So tell me how things are going here," he asked Morris. "It's quieter, what with only me and the Mrs. here," stated Morris. Then turning to Gina and Arthur, Bill asked how they are finding their classes in college," Gina had a lot to say and was so excited to tell Bill everything that she fumbled with her words. Arthur was a bit surer of himself, but they both were a bit nervous. Mrs. Locke and Gina offered to take Liz on a short tour of the manor while the men went outside to look at some of the ideas Arthur had for improving things at the manor. While they were walking around, Morris asked if there was any news of Mr. Chestermere. All Bill said was that Mr. Chestermere had settled into his scheduled routine. He mentioned that they shouldn't be concerned with him. He was out of their lives.

Bill turned to Arthur and said, "I see you have some excellent ideas. I wish you luck." Mr. Locke added that what Arthur planned would add to the manor's value. He and Mrs. Locke will support him and Gina wholeheartedly.

Looking at his watch, Bill said he and Liz must be on their way. They met Liz and the ladies on the curved front steps under the portico since it had started to rain. Their goodbyes were pleasant. Margaret was trying not to show she was crying. "They are such a nice couple, and it was too bad how we met him, but I'm glad we did."

In two days, it would be Christmas, and Gina was excited, about whether her parents would like her gift, but she also felt sad that soon she would be going back to college. Jr. would be stopping by the day after New Year's Day to drive her back to London. Gina looked forward to that. She was a little nervous, knowing how she felt about Jr. and not knowing if he felt the same. She knows she will enjoy her time alone with Jr.

Christmas Day was a wonderful time at the Manor. With all the decorations that they put up and the beautifully decorated tree, it will be one Christmas neither of them would forget. Mr. & Mrs. Locke loved the picture of Big Ben that Gina drew. Her parents gave her a sweater that her mother made that brought out the flecks in her hazel eyes. Gina gave Arthur a book on botany that he had been looking at at the college, and her parents gave him a pen set with his initials. Arthur gave Gina a book of drawings by famous artists. The dinner was wonderful. With fresh vegetables from the garden, as well as a delicious turkey, Mrs. Locke outdid herself. She planned to give Gina and Arthur each a care package to bring back to college. She even prepared a small one for Jr.

The day after Boxing Day, the Lockes and Arthur went to put some flowers on the Beavingtons graves. Having worked for the Beavingtons for almost 20 years, the Lockes cared for them like they were family; even Arthur felt close to them in the short time he worked at the manor. They had planned to landscape the gravesites with a few of their favorite plants, those that could withstand the seasons. Arthur didn't pay much attention to what Henry did with the landscaping, but with the knowledge he is learning in class, they will be able to choose correctly.

CHAPTER 3

While Gina and Arthur settled down to an academic routine, Mr. Chestermere also had to follow a scheduled routine. He had to rise at 7 a.m. and be in the dining room for breakfast at 7:30 a.m. After breakfast, there were scheduled activities that each resident had to participate in. Attending was mandatory unless a resident was ill or had an appointment with the hospital director. The activities were set up for mind and body development. Nothing was too strenuous. There are also exercise classes planned, but they would only be for physically capable residents. Since the hospital was small, it housed 100 residents; some residents were involved in the activities while others are expected to join in the group therapy session. Some activities included puzzles of all sorts, and word games, like scrabble. Then an hour later, those residents who were in the activities session went to group therapy, and those who were in group therapy became involved in the activities session. After morning sessions, they had lunch, and if not scheduled for an appointment, they had free time until 6 p.m., dinner time. A resident could go outside into the courtyard for fresh air. Staff regularly walked around, keeping an eye on everyone. The courtyard was a charming area, with seating areas surrounded by small shrubs and a variety of flowers, some of which Henry could identify. He could easily see that the groundsman cared about his work. He asked the director if he could help out in the care of the plants. Still, because of the chemicals used and considering what Henry used in the murders, the director decided it would not be a good idea, but that Henry could talk with the gardeners when they're out working. Henry did understand the director's reasoning.

At first, Mr. Chestermere would not join any session, but after a long talk with Dr. Wilson, the director, he suggested that Henry join the sessions. After all, he was required to send a progress report to the courts detailing his progress. If satisfactory, he would be eligible to receive visitors after six months and qualify for the escorted day trips after three months. Jr. had visited the director to follow up on Mr. Chestermere's progress. It was a visit Jr. would not want to repeat. He would have one of the junior staff to make the monthly visits. Jr. could not mention his visit to Gina as it was a private affair.

The staff noticed that Henry did not communicate with other residents unless directly approached. But, there was one other resident that he did have something in common with. His name is Harry Stratton, who had also fought during the Suez Crisis. They did not tell each other what they were in for, as they were both ashamed of their actions. The staff brought this "friendship" up to the director, who advised them to keep an eye on them. But as the "friendship" progressed, Henry was calmer and participated in the scheduled activity time. He had a feeling of being watched, especially when he was talking with Harry. He knew that the staff observed their actions because they had to make a report to the director. He told Harry that it could look suspicious if they are together too often, especially now that they both confided in each other that they want to escape. Henry decided he will be the model of good behavior by actively participating in all scheduled classes, even though he found most of them boring. He desperately wants to go out on a day trip. Only four residents and two staff go each time, and Henry wants to be one of the four. Two days before a scheduled trip, the names of those to be going were announced, and Henry was one of them. He was quite happy, and he hadn't felt like that since he arrived there. Harry would not be going because he had an altercation with one of the staff, so he must now be on his best behavior in hopes of being chosen for the next trip, which will be in one month. A resident going on this trip would not be able to go again until the one after the next one.

Henry found that if he followed the rules with no complaints, then he got favorable results on his report to the director. He figured that was the way to get considered for the day trips. He would keep his nose clean and sort of fade into the background. He noticed that anyone who made a scene would be more closely watched by staff. He even decided that he would continue to take the medications given to him until he found a way around it.

About a month after his arrival at the hospital, Henry asked the director for any news of the people at the manor. The director told him that he was instructed not to give any information out about the manor and that it didn't concern him anymore. That fact upset Henry, but he realized there was nothing he could do about it, so he calmly accepted the director's word. But, deep down, he still wanted to know how he could find out anything. He felt it was a good sign when he befriended Harry, who told him that his sister has a friend who lives in Cockernhoe, and he would ask her if she could get information for him.

The time for the day trip is looming, and Henry is excited about it. They would be going to the famous London museum and for a light luncheon afterward at a nearby café. The residents were reminded beforehand not to stray from the group and to be respectful to others. When the day arrived, Henry tried not to look too excited. He didn't want to draw too much attention to himself.

Much to his surprise, Henry found that he enjoyed the visit to the museum. He had been there when he was attending university and noticed the many changes. Before he realized it, it was time for the luncheon, which was also enjoyable. The various foods to sample were a welcome change from the hospital meals.

Arriving back at the hospital, they had some free time. Henry sought out Harry and filled him in about his trip to the museum and the excellent luncheon afterward. Harry did not seem very interested; he was upset he did not get to go. Maybe next time encourages Henry. "When is your sister coming to visit you next?" asked Henry with anticipation. "Not until next week," mentioned Harry. "She has to arrange for time off work and someone to care for her young sons." "You won't forget to ask her if she would be able to get some information from her friend who lives in Cockernhoe, would you?" Henry reminded Harry. "And what did you say her friend's name was?" Henry asked. "Yes, yes, I told you I would," mumbled Harry, "her name is Dorothy, and you don't have to keep reminding me, what do you think I am, daft or something."

He yelled. "Quiet," murmured Henry, "the staff are watching." "Bugger, the staff," shouted Harry. "They can all go to hell for all I care." "Just calm down," insisted Henry then he left the room. "If Harry gets so upset over something that simple, I wonder if I will be able to count on him when the time comes for our escape," Henry thought to himself. After dinner, Henry went to the library, took out a book, and pretended to read, but he is contemplating their escape plan. For the escape to happen successfully, we both have to go on the day trip at the same time. It wouldn't do for us to escape individually. Security would be tightened up, and the day trips would probably be put on hold for a while. Henry decided to observe Harry's behavior for the next few weeks to see if this was only a one-time occurrence of his rage towards the staff.

Much to his surprise, Henry is now getting used to the scheduled days. It reminds him of his training for the Suez Crisis. He finds it comforting to have a routine, even though he would rather it not be in this place.

Sometimes during the free time, Henry still finds himself thinking about the manor, mostly about the grounds, since he put so much of his time and energy into them. He doesn't think badly of the Lockes, he did find them easy to get along with, even Gina. There could not be better people living at the manor especially if he can't be there.

A week later, Harry's sister, Helen, came for a visit and was able to tell Harry that her friend's daughter Trisha is the girl Mrs. Locke hired to help at the manor a few times and was so impressed with her that she promised Trisha that she would need help come planting time. Mrs. Locke wanted a bigger garden than they previously had, and she thought that it was a great idea when Gina suggested that they give some extra produce to needy families in Cockernhoe. Helen asked Dorothy that maybe Trisha could keep an ear open about what's happening at the manor. Dorothy knew Trisha was happy to get the work, so she advised her to be discreet when she talks to Mrs. Locke about what's going on at the manor. Henry was so thankful that Helen was able to be of some help. He remembered Dorothy and knows that her circumstances are not to her liking, so he figured if he was to mention the possibility of a monetary nature that Dorothy would help as much as she could. It would just be a matter of Dorothy and Trisha being discreet. Henry wondered if he wrote her a letter pointing out the fact that he could help her with her financial needs if that would entice her to help. He'll ask

Harry to give it to Helen, and she could pass it on to Dorothy. And, of course, Harry requested that Henry consider offering his sister money also, even though he knows Helen receives money from his account to cover costs of bus fare and child care when she visits. Henry agreed that he would but after he hears from Dorothy's. He must, therefore, wait patiently not to arouse suspicion and not let anyone notice any change in his behavior. Once he knows that Helen and Dorothy are on board, he could then make further plans. He will try to put his name in for another day trip, but since he recently went on one, he may not be considered for another one so soon. But, he figured since the manor is not going to go anywhere, he has time to be more precise in his planning.

Henry confided in Harry that he knew Dorothy when he lived in Cockernhoe. She was about ten years younger than him and was married to a lazy man. Dorothy had a child (assuming it must be Trisha), and she had to work at whatever job she could get because of her lazy husband.

CHAPTER 4

With Christmas and New Years over, it was time for Gina to return to London. Arthur left a few days earlier to spend some time with his mother and grandmother. Jr. Keyes would be arriving later that day and would stay the night as a guest of the manor and then drive to London. He would be driving Gina back to college. This way, they could have some time alone before going back to their routines. Gina had a great time visiting her parents but is anxious to get back to her classes.

When Jr. arrived at the manor, he was happy to see Gina was alone while waiting for him. He ran up the stairs and gave Gina a big hug and a quick kiss, and because he did that, it gave Gina the answer to her earlier question to her mother, whether or not Jr. thought of her as a girlfriend.

When they got to London, Jr. told Gina he had a surprise for her. He took her to a fancy restaurant for dinner, where she felt she wasn't appropriately dressed, but Jr. assured her that she looked great. He had booked a private room for their dinner. "Wow," says Gina, "I have walked by this place a lot, but never thought I could ever afford to eat here. Are you sure it's not too expensive?" Jr. told her it was a special occasion, and he wanted the best for their "first date" as boyfriend and girlfriend. Seeing the look on Gina's face, Jr. said, "Yes, Gina, I would like us to be boyfriend and girlfriend. I like you very much and would like to spend more time with you, time permitting, with your class schedule. What do you think?" he asked. "I would like that a lot," whispered Gina. "I like you very much also," she added shyly. "So, to seal the deal, so to speak," announces Jr. "I have a present for you." "You didn't have to buy me a present," protested Gina. "I have one for you also, but it's in my luggage in the car." "You can give it to me tomorrow," stated Jr. "I want to take you out for breakfast if that's okay with you." "I would love that," answered Gina. "Now, would you like to open my present?" he asks. Gina tried to open the gift without tearing the gift wrap, but her hands are shaking so much that she only ends up tearing it. Finally, she got the box open and exclaimed! "it's beautiful," as she lifted out the key chain of Big Ben. "Thank you so much," she gushed. She didn't want this evening to end, so she asked him a lot of questions about his parents and France. Jr. was pleased that Gina was taking an interest in his parents. "That must mean she likes me more than just as a friend," he thought to himself. It's soon time to leave the restaurant and head over to Arthur's grandmother's house. As they pull up at Arthur's grandmother's house, Jr. gave Gina a quick kiss on her lips. And Gina kissed him back with a dreamy look in her eyes. She wondered if this is what it felt like to be in love.

CHAPTER 5

Since Helen was from Rumforton and Dorothy from Cockernhoe, they both knew why Henry was in Bethlehem Royal Hospital. Helen wasn't sure Harry should befriend him. As far as she was concerned, his crime was not as severe as murder, even though a boy had died as a result of Harry's actions. So when Helen told Dorothy what Henry wanted, she also told her to keep it confidential. Helen didn't think it would be wrong to pass on any information about the manor folks as long as it wasn't anything personal. All Henry wanted was to be kept up to date of the people at the manor. "It's too bad things turned out this way," she confided to Dorothy. "Are you sure we can't get into trouble for doing this?" Dorothy asked Helen. "No," responded Helen, "It would just be idle gossip. You knew Henry from the village, what did you think of him?" asked Helen. "I found him rather aloof like he thought he was better than everyone else in the village," added Dorothy. "But he was about ten years older than me."

"All you need to do is ask Trisha from time to time how things are going at the manor and how everyone is doing," Helen suggested to Dorothy. "She doesn't have to snoop into their private things or anything, just repeat to you what she and Mrs. Locke talk about," added Helen. "Does Trisha know of our friendship?" "Trisha might think you're interested and just being curious," said Dorothy. "As are many people in the village, and some are surprised that such a quiet man could do such a thing." "When do you go visit Harry again?" asked Dorothy. "In a fortnight," answered Helen. "I just need someone to watch over the kids once they come home from school." "I can probably do it for you," Dorothy said thoughtfully, "I can let Trisha know I won't be home and she could watch out for her brothers when they get home from school. I can be here by 2:30, would that be okay?" she asked. "Are you sure Trisha won't mind?" Helen asked, "I would appreciate it very muChapter Harry has called at least three times this week alone, and it is becoming very annoying." "Oh no, it will be okay with Trisha. She can get the boys a snack and put them in front of the telly, while she works on her homework," added Dorothy. "What time do you think you would be coming back? When are visiting hours over?" Dorothy asked. "If I get to London for the 11 a.m. visiting time, I could catch the 3 p.m. bus back this way," added Helen. "I would be home by 5 p.m., there would be no need for you to feed them, all you need to do is give them a snack after school, and they will be fine until tea time. I can't tell you how much I appreciate it," added Helen.

CHAPTER 6

Back on campus, Gina and several friends met for tea and talked about their Christmas holidays. There were so many happy memories shared. The majority of her fellow students were from London and lived at home, so going away did not mean as much to them as it did for Gina. To them, their Christmas break was not as exciting as those who came from smaller towns or villages, like Gina. Everyone seemed anxious to get on with their studies and find out how they did on their mid-terms.

Gina was so excited about her "date" with Jr. and also about the good marks she got that she wrote to her mother as soon as she could. She does not yet have a close enough friend at college that she felt she could confide in about Jr. There is one girl who is quite shy, that she had spoken to a few times. Gina planned to invite her to go for a tea to get to know more about her. She thought that no-one should be alone and felt that she and Eloise could be friends.

The day before classes resumed, Gina had lunch with Arthur. They enjoyed reminiscing about the manor and their New Years' celebrations. Arthur was also happy with the marks he got and is as anxious as Gina is to continue classes.

There was one other reason Arthur was anxious to start classes. He had gotten to know a girl in one of his classes, whom he liked and would like to get to know her better. Before the holidays, they had a chance to talk, and each confessed to the other that there is a mutual attraction between them. Her name is Christine, and she is from Kirkcudbright, a small town about 72 miles from Glasgow, Scotland. She was attending college in London because there was no college in her hometown that offered the courses she needed. She could have attended in Glasgow, but her parents thought that her studying in London would be a life-changing experience for her. She just got back to campus late the night before classes were to resume, so Arthur hadn't an opportunity to talk to her, but he did find a note attached to his dorm room from her arranging to meet during their spare period. He decided not to tell Gina for fear of jinxing things.

With the start of the new semester, Gina and Arthur both have different classes so that they won't be seeing as much of each other as before. They do have a standing arrangement to meet each Sunday morning for church services. Then they go to Arthur's grandmothers for lunch unless Gina had a date with Jr. Arthur would like his mother and grandmother to meet Christine, but he wanted to get to know her better first. He didn't want to scare her away, but since her family is in Scotland, he felt she could use a mother figure, which could be either his mother or grandmother. He's sure that once they know about Christine, they would insist he invite her to lunch.

Arthur's grandmother teasingly asked him if he is sweet on anyone at college. When they saw him blush, they knew it was true. With a bit of coaxing, he told them about Christine. As he guessed, they wanted to meet her. His mother suggested that Arthur bring her for Sunday dinner next week. They also told Gina to invite Jr...

CHAPTER 7

After witnessing another of Harry's altercations with an attendant, Henry was having doubts that he confided in him of his escape plans. He felt that he would have to appease Harry at times in the hopes that he would not brag about the fact that he may be leaving soon. Henry would have to trust that if Harry said anything that the staff would put it down to his mental issues. Other patients had mentioned that Harry's behavior runs hot and cold; one can never trust him. Henry vowed to keep a close watch on him. If it got worse, Henry would mention that he has decided not to try to escape so that Harry wouldn't betray him. He would tell him it was just a thought, but that he has now accepted his fate, and it didn't seem such a bad place to be. One day when Harry was feeling calm, he observed Henry and wondered if he would try to exclude him from his escape plans. Even though he knows that Henry is in for murder, he is not afraid of him. If Henry decided to renege on his plan to take him with him, Harry believed he can do it on his own.

After six months and with good behavior, Henry would be able to receive visitors. He would have to submit a list of people he wanted to visit him or who he would like to see, and then if they checked out, Henry would be allowed to send a permission slip for them to fill out and return before any visits would be scheduled.

He didn't make many friends or acquaintances as he was growing up that he could think of who might want to visit him, and he didn't keep in touch with anyone from college or the army, but he might submit Mr. Locke's name and Arthurs. He doesn't as yet know that Arthur and Gina are co-inheritors. He had no idea even if they would want to visit him, but he thought it would be a way to find out what is going on at the manor. He also wondered if it would be a good idea to submit Dorothy's name since they both lived in Cockernhoe; they weren't friends, but the authorities don't need to know the extent of their relationship. After all, he is about ten years older than Dorothy, and they did not associate with each other since Henry was a loner; also, Dorothy's husband was a jealous, lazy man. Now that Henry knows that Dorothy's husband was no longer living with her, he felt it would be easier to be in contact with her, even if it is through Helen for now.

CHAPTER 8

Back home in Cockernhoe, Mr. & Mrs. Locke were keeping the manor up, which wasn't too much work, since they are the only ones living there; and it being the winter season, there was not a lot of outdoor work to do. They received a postcard from DS Dunes and his wife, who are enjoying their honeymoon. They would be coming through Cockernhoe on their return journey and asked if they could stop for tea. Mrs. Locke was touched that they remembered them and is now planning the tea. Her husband hoped she didn't go to too much trouble. She would like to discuss the upcoming visit with Gina, but since classes resumed, Gina and Arthur won't be coming home every weekend. Not only is their class schedule more intense, but they both are also in relationships they want to grow. Mrs. Locke would tell Gina on her weekly phone call home. Gina promised to write to her parents weekly, even though they talk on the phone. This way, she could go into more detail about her news, especially about her growing relationship with Jr. She knows Arthur is seeing someone, even though he hasn't said anything. Gina had seen them together on campus, and she could tell they weren't just classmates. She mentioned this in a letter to her mom but told her not to say a word to anyone, even her father.

With the two kids gone, Mrs. Locke has felt lonely at times. She had invited Trisha's mother to tea once or twice. Even with their age difference, they have a common bond of both being mothers. Mr. &

Mrs. Locke knew Dorothy's husband and are glad he had left, even though it is a struggle for Dorothy as a single parent. Trisha brings home some money when she helped at the manor. She comes on the weekends. A few times, she brought her younger brothers, who follow Mr. Locke around the grounds, continually asking questions. He found he enjoyed those visits. If Henry knew that Dorothy is close to Mrs. Locke, he felt sure of his decision to submit her name for someone he would like to have visit him

CHAPTER 9

Gina was finding her classes very interesting. She was making friends of classmates and others around the campus. Since her grades are above average, Gina didn't feel as pressured as some of her classmates to spend more time studying. She felt confident that the time she spent with Jr. didn't affect her grades because she enjoyed those times and would not want to jeopardize what she felt was a growing relationship or her studies. With the spring break looming, the students were concentrating on their studies for the mid-term exam before the two-week break. Gina would be going home and was looking forward to it, but her main priority was her exams. Her relationship with Jr. comes in at a close second. Since London is only an hour's drive away, Gina knew that Jr. would be able to come to the manor over the spring break, so she was not too worried about having a bit less time to spend with him now. She really missed her parents and the manor quite a lot.

Just as Gina was looking forward to spring break, so was Arthur. His marks are also above average, and he was also not as worried as some of his classmates seemed to be. He planned to go out to the manor for the first week, and then he would go back to London to spend the last week with his mother and grandmother.

Gina and Arthur have both matured since starting college. For Gina, it was a bit more overwhelming than for Arthur. She had only been to London a few times in her life and only for short visits.

There were so many people, and everyone seemed to be in a hurry. There had been several times when Gina found herself just stopping on the sidewalk to take a breath. Will she ever get used to it, she wondered? It did help when she went out with Jr. He made it look so easy to get around. He said that by the time Gina has finished college, she would be feeling and acting just like a local.

But not Arthur, he knows his way around London because his mother and grandmother live there and he visited regularly. He was the perfect tour guide for Christine, who was from a small town in Scotland.

She told her parents that she met a nice guy in one of her classes, whom she liked a lot and felt that he returned the feelings. She explained that he is from out of London, but that his mother and grandmother lived in London.

CHAPTER 10

Henry received the good news that he could receive visitors and that he should make a list of those he wanted as visitors. He decided to add Mr. Locke's and Sr. Keyes's names (he doesn't know that Sr. Keyes is now retired in France and that Jr. is in charge). He also decided to add Dorothy's name. Having to think of names to submit had made Henry think about his life up to now. Of his classmates in college, he did not have anyone he could consider a close friend. He always was a loner, even during the Suez Crisis. Now he wished he had attempted to make a few friends, but that's the past, and there is no way to change it. He was happy being alone, and at the time he associated with people like the Beavingtons and Lockes, that was enough socializing for him. He must admit, he did like Arthur. He found him to be polite and a quick learner. He would add Arthur's name to the list. He did hope Arthur was still helping at the manor and that he would continue in the same line of studies. He felt that Arthur had the knack for such work.

Henry had been told that the process for checking the names on his list did not take long. Next, he would have to write to each approved person asking if they would visit him. He was unsure if any of his choices would consider his request. Henry would very much like to talk to someone who has a clear mind, or as some residents put it, "someone who is not bonkers." He found his conversations with the resident psychiatrist relaxing. After their scheduled time, Henry stayed a few more minutes, and they would have a regular conversation, almost as if they were friends. Henry felt he would undoubtedly like to have a friend or two; maybe when he finally got released, he would socialize more. Of course, there is no talk of when that will be, if ever. After all, his sentence was for life. He would do his best to be a perfect resident so he can be chosen for day trips and not have the attendants continually watching his every move. That could make a person paranoid. He learned discipline in the army, so he will now attempt to get back into that frame of mind.

CHAPTER 11

Gina was friendly with most of her classmates but had noticed that there was one person, his name was George, who always seems to be around when she is. She realizes that he was taking the same classes as she is except for the estate management class, so he was bound to be where she is. But why did she get a nervous feeling when she saw him out of class? Her friend Eloise also noticed his presence and came to the same conclusion as Gina. But, when he would happen to be there after her management class and when she and Eloise would be leaving their dorm on their way to the cafeteria, it was making Gina nervous. She asked Eloise if maybe she imagined things, but Eloise said she felt the same. "It's creepy, don't you think," mentioned Eloise, as they were going to the cafeteria for a study session over their favorite coffee and snack. "Do you think we should say something to one of the professors?" she asked Gina. "I'm not sure, but I will mention it to my friend, Arthur, and see what he thinks we should do before involving a professor. After all, if it's just coincidence, I don't want to get George into trouble. I'll talk to Arthur on Sunday on our way back from his grandmother's. In the meantime, let's get studying," she added. As the girls dug into their snacks and books, they did not see George peeking through the café window.

At the other college cafeteria, Arthur and Christine were also studying and enjoying tea and snacks. Arthur was mostly daydreaming. Christine was telling him a story about when she was six years old when she got lost while visiting her grandparent's farm in the highlands. She was out exploring with her older sister and younger brother. Her brother had fallen and skinned his knee and made such a fuss that her older sister decided to take him home for grandma to care for it. Christine didn't want to go back yet, so her sister told her to wait there, and she would be right back. It had seemed like she was waiting a long time and was starting to feel frightened, so she tried to make her way back by herself but soon realized that she did not know which way to go. As she remembered how scared she was, her eyes widened, and Arthur would swear it made him feel he was right there with her.

On Sunday, Arthur and Christine went to church with Gina, and Jr. picked them up afterward to go for the usual Sunday dinner at Arthur's grandmother's home. Christine confided in Arthur that she was feeling nervous but is also looking forward to meeting Arthur's mother, and his grandmother, Daphne, and having Sunday lunch with everyone. She had heard so much about them from Arthur that she felt she knew them already. She mentioned that she was just as nervous when she met Gina and Jr. last week. Of course, there was no need to worry at all; Maggie and Daphne were so welcoming; that she felt at home right away. It made her momentarily miss her family back home. His grandmother asked Christine if she would be going home for the spring break. Christine told her that for personal reasons, she would be staying at college for the break. "No, no, my dear, I will not hear of it," announced Daphne. She told Christine that she would be more than welcome to stay with them. Christine thanked her and told her that she would write to her parents to let them know of her plans. On the way back to college, Christine said to the others that she had a wonderful time and that she felt welcomed. Christine called her parents and explained the situation. She asked them if they would be able to come to London during her spring break. When they said no, she told them about the invitation from Arthur's grandmother and mother to stay a week and then was invited by Gina to spend the last week of spring break in Cockernhoe. Even though Gina had just met Christine, she felt like she has known her for much longer. Gina had always wanted to have a sister.

After Jr. dropped them off at the college, Gina took a moment to ask Arthur if she could talk to him for a moment. He said goodnight to Christine, and he and Gina went into the lounge. She told him how she and Eloise felt when they are continually noticing George was always around where they are and wondered what to do about it. "Which one is George?" Arthur asked. "He's the tall guy with red hair and wire glasses," added Gina. "I know who you mean," stated Arthur. "He seemed like a quiet guy, and from what I saw of any interaction he has had with other female classmates, he was always courteous." "What do you think I should do," asked Gina. "He gives Eloise and me the creeps." "Try not ever to be alone with him if you feel like that," added Arthur. "But if you feel it is not a coincidence, let me know, and maybe I can talk to him," added Arthur. "As you mentioned, if it is innocent, then we don't want to get him into trouble."

CHAPTER 12

At the manor, Mrs. Locke was again running around in a fluster. Bill Dunes and his wife will be stopping at the manor on their way back to London. Mr. Locke had offered to help, but as most women know, men cannot clean as well as a woman can, so he was relegated to making sure the grounds were immaculate. "Why must you do so much when it is just a short visit," he asked his wife. "A person never knows what may occur, my dear Mr. Locke," his wife responded. "One must be prepared for anything. It is what we learned from our mothers and what they learned from their mothers. I still have my copy of Mrs. Beeton's Book of Household Management that was handed down from my grandmother. I intend to present it to Gina when she takes over her inheritance." "But getting back to my question, why so much fuss for just a short visit?" puts in Mr. Locke. "You don't understand, my dear Mr. Locke, with Gina and Arthur away, I need something to do, so the upcoming visit from DS Dunes and his dear bride will be just the thing so I will feel needed," she added. "But I need you," Mr. Locke stated. "I know, my dear, you need me, but I am accustomed to doing more and am finding it hard to keep myself occupied. I hope you can understand," pleaded Mrs. Locke. "I do," added Mr. Locke. "I am also finding myself at odds."

"I am counting the days when Gina will be home for spring break. I am sure she hasn't been eating properly, didn't you think she looked a bit thin when she was here for Christmas," Mrs. Locke asked her husband. "She looked fine to me, mother," added Mr. Locke. "You worry too much."

"I am so proud of our Gina, aren't you," Mrs. Locke asked her husband. "You bet I am," he replied. "And I am equally proud of Arthur," he added. "With what those two had to experience at such a young age, they are both doing well. This manor will be under excellent management when they have graduated from college and put their knowledge into play. Mother, he added, this place will be vibrating with joy soon."

"So now when did you say that DS Dunes would be arriving," he asked. "They should be here Friday at about 2 p.m.," answered Mrs. Locke. "Is there anything you need my help with," he asked. "No, thank you," replied Mrs. Locke. "Everything is ready, we can have a relaxing day tomorrow, but Friday morning, I will want to make sure everything is as it should be," she added.

CHAPTER 13

G ina and Eloise hadn't noticed George in their vicinity since they told Arthur about him. They both felt a bit foolish thinking he was up to something, but they should always be careful when out, especially alone. They forgot about him as they attended classes as usual and went for tea from time to time. Then one day, when Gina was walking alone from the library to her dorm, she felt sure that someone was following her, but every time she turned around, there were so many students around that she felt foolish thinking it was George. When she got to her dorm, she went to see Eloise and told her, and she can still feel the goosebumps. It must be that I'm tired she said to herself and just imagined it. Eloise suggested that they try to walk together as much as they could. With exams looming, Gina pushed the thought of George from her mind and tackled her books.

Gina, Eloise, Arthur, and Christine had made plans to go to a local deli for a celebration after their last exams before going their separate ways for the two-week break. They agreed that they had enough of college cafeteria food and could splurge at their celebration tea. They were so engrossed in their plans that no- one noticed George lingering behind the lilac bush.

Christine had talked to her parents, and they agreed that she could stay at Daphne's for the first week and with Gina in Cockernhoe for the last week, but they would like to talk to Arthur's grandmother and Gina's parents first. She and Arthur will drive down to Cockernhoe together. Christine is looking forward to seeing more English countryside and staying in a real manor house.

Since George was a classmate in one of Christine's classes and she found him to be a nice guy, so when he asked her what her plans were for the spring break, she told him about staying in London for a week, then going with Arthur to stay at Cockernhoe for the last week. "Isn't Gina from Cockernhoe," he then asked? "Yes, Arthur, also," she replied. "Is Eloise going too," he asked? "No, she will stay in London; her cousins will be visiting," Christine answered. "Would you like to go for a coffee," he asked. "Sorry, I can't, I'm waiting for someone, thanks anyway," she answered. "I hope you enjoy the break, and good luck with the finals," he added as he left. Christine sees Arthur has a puzzled look on his face. "Is something wrong," she asked him? "Was that George I saw you talking to?" he inquired. "I didn't know you knew him," "Yes," replied Christine, "he's in my literature class." "What did he want," he asked? "He just asked what I would be doing during spring break and wished me luck on my finals. Why do you ask?" she added. "Do you know him?" "Yes, I have met him. Please forgive me, I felt a small pang of jealousy," admitted Arthur. "No problem," stated Christine. "Are we going for tea now?" "You bet," he added as he takes her hand.

CHAPTER 14

Henry made his list of possible visitors and wrote the required letters asking those on his list if they would visit him. The director told him that once he checked out the names, he would then send the messages that Henry wrote. As Henry anxiously awaited the results of his letters, he continued going to the library during his free time to read anything he can about being a lord of a manor. The staff noticed the many visits Henry made to the library and brought this to the attention of the director. The director felt that the solicitors should inform Henry about the Forfeiture Act. Even though Henry deserved what happened to him, the director felt that it was cruel to let him go on thinking that he was still lord of the manor. The director consulted with the resident psychiatrist about how to bring the news to Henry and if Henry would be stable enough to hear the news.

On the one hand, letting Henry believe he is still lord of the manor gave him something positive to focus on, and he is doing quite well in his sessions. But, telling him he is no longer the lord of the manor can trigger a reversal of his behavior, and he could become very negative. The director decided to talk to the solicitor and a representative of the court before he makes a final decision.

The director observed Henry in contact with other patients and was pleased with what he saw. Henry was kind and considerate to others and, in one case, even helped another patient who had dropped a deck of cards and was starting to get upset, but when Henry offered to help her, she relaxed quite quickly. The director knew that that specific patient is usually hard to get to calm down without a shot of some relaxing agent by an attendant.

The director made an appointment with Henry's solicitor to report on his behavior and to get the solicitor's opinion on whether to inform Henry about the Forfeiture Act.

Meanwhile, all the names on the list Henry gave him for visitors checked out. He informed Henry that he would send out his letters of request. Henry was a bit nervous about the message to the Lockes and the one he wrote to Dorothy. He wasn't sure how they felt about him now. He would understand if they did not want to be a visitor; the same went for Arthur. All he can do was write those letters and wait for any responses.

Henry also tried to be sure to remain on friendly terms with Harry. Although they don't talk about their dream of escaping anymore, he knew Harry would like to.

CHAPTER 15

The mid-term exams were finally over. Gina, Arthur, Christine, and Eloise met at the rotunda and are on their way to their celebratory tea. Arthur commented that he is glad the exams were over, and he is a fortunate guy to be in the company of three such attractive ladies. Gina told them that Jr. would be picking her up soon, and they would head out to the manor. Jr. would only be able to stay the weekend. Arthur and Christine then leave for his grandmother's house. As Eloise leaves she thanks Gina again for the invitation and regrets that she won't be able to visit the manor. Since both her parents work, she is needed to watch over her younger siblings while they are off school for reading week, and also, her cousins would be visiting from Chelsea.

Christine mentioned her conversation with George and asked if they knew him. "Why do you ask," commented Gina as she looked searchingly at Eloise and Arthur. "Do you know him? Is he in one of your classes?" asked Gina. "What did he want?" "Yes, he's in my literature class," responded Christine. "He was asking if I would be going home for the spring break, and what your plans were and Arthur's. He also asked if Eloise will be going to Cockernhoe." "Why are you looking like that? Did I do something wrong?" Christine asked. "Not really, you weren't to know," Arthur added. "It's just that he seemed to freak Gina and Eloise out. They would notice him hanging around wherever they would be." "But, since he does attend college here and is probably in some of their classes, it would be perfectly natural that they would see him quite frequently," stated Christine. "We may just be imagining it, but it just gave us the creeps to see him peeking in the café window or coming out from behind a bush as we walked by. It may be nothing," shrugged Gina. "Maybe we were feeling the stress of the coming mid-terms. At least there is no chance I would be seeing him at the manor."

After everyone had left, Gina sat in the rotunda, waiting for Jr. She was so anxious to get home that she didn't notice George at the other end of the rotunda, sitting on a bench hidden by a huge bush. Just as George started walking toward Gina, Jr. pulled up in his fancy car. He jumped out of the vehicle to help Gina with her bags. After giving her a quick kiss on her cheek, they drive off. If Gina had turned around at that moment, she would have seen George staring after them.

CHAPTER 16

A t the manor, Mrs. Locke had her husband rushing around working on the finishing touches in her preparation for when Gina and Jr. arrive. They were both excited about Gina's two-week break. They would only have part of a week with Gina since Jr. will be staying two days, and then Arthur and Christine will be spending the last week at the manor. Mr. and Mrs. Locke were anxious to meet Christine. Mrs. Locke wanted to have Trisha and her mother over for tea one day while Gina and Arthur were home.

Not only are the Lockes looking forward to the spring break, so was Gina, Arthur, and Christine. Mr. and Mrs. Locke had a pleasant conversation with Christine's parents and assured them that Christine was very welcome. The more, the merrier Mrs. Locke told Christine's mother. It would be like old times when there were young people around. A place the size of the manor needs more people to make it feel merrier.

Gina and Arthur both planned to start on some of their ideas. Gina will begin preparing the garden, and Arthur hoped to get at least one chicken coop built so Mr. Locke can go out and buy some chicks.

Arthur had an idea for a surprise for Gina. He wanted her to have a studio but isn't sure if one of the many rooms in the manor can be turned into a studio, or maybe he could build one near the gardens. He hoped to have a few moments alone with the Lockes to ask their opinion.

CHAPTER 17

The departure of her friends to their respective destinations left Eloise feeling lonely. Jr. was driving Gina home, and he would be staying for a couple of nights. Arthur and Christine left for his grandmother's house, where they will remain for the first week, then go to Cockernhoe for the remaining week. As Eloise was on her way to catch the bus, she thought she saw George lingering behind the fragrant sweet box shrubs. He started walking toward her, but her bus arrived, and she boarded, breathing a sigh of relief. He still gave her the creeps.

George was a bit put out that he didn't have time to talk to Eloise before her bus arrived. He wanted to ask her if she would like to go for tea, and then he would work the conversation around to seeing her home. He knew where Gina lived but didn't think he would have a reliable excuse if he went there and happened to run into her or Arthur. He would have to wait until classes resume before he attempted to befriend Gina. Maybe he could get Gina's phone number from Eloise. He would have to be friendly to her so she would feel comfortable giving it to him. Little did he realize that Eloise thought he was creepy, so his chances of her being comfortable around him were slim to none. It's a good thing that he managed to get Eloise's phone number from one of her classmates. He used the excuse that he was part of their study group and needed her number because he was in charge of arranging one of those study nights but had lost her number.

George felt that it was fate that he should get to know Gina as more than a classmate. It was the same feeling he had for that other girl at the previous college. Gina was the only one who was kind to him on registration day. He had dropped his papers and looked so lost, as lost as she felt herself. She helped him pick up his papers and attempted to point him in the right direction. When he looked into her eyes, they reminded him of his mother's and aunt's eyes. He felt a connection with her, and now he spent a lot of his time dreaming about her. He wanted to be near her at all times. It's a good thing that he was in several of her classes. He had tried to change one of his other classes so he could be in most of her classes, but it was too late in the semester for him to change. He would like to be able to talk with her alone, but whenever he saw her, she was with someone else. As he boarded his bus to his aunt's house, he decided he would wait a couple of days before phoning Eloise. He really must not make the same mistakes he made at the other college. His uncle had to assure the dean at Croydon that the incident at the previous college was just a misunderstanding, but in order for the parents not to press charges, George had to leave. George's uncle warned him that he better not have a repeat of his behavior at this college and that he needed the education to pursue a career. By the time his bus arrived at his stop, George had been mumbling to himself and creeping out other passengers.

CHAPTER 18

Henry was doing well at Bethlehem. The attendants had noticed that he is calmer and would be one of the first to help another resident during craft sessions. Even during personal time, Henry could be seen conversing with others, something he had never done before. The attendants also noticed that even Harry seemed calmer.

Henry knew that Harry was impatient about when they might try to escape. He told Harry that they must be patient, that they must not show they are anxious about anything. That would tip off the attendants, and then they would be watching them more closely. He told Harry that they have to plan carefully and think of anything that might go wrong. He told Harry not to worry. The attendants are probably reporting back to the director about how calm they are and their good behavior, which was a good thing. But they must act calmly and not show that anything is bothering them; and if it was noticed by the attendants, it would mean they wouldn't be under such strict observation. Henry mentioned that he was feeling comfortable here, but is anxiously waiting for the responses from those he wrote to ask if they would visit him. His solicitor's office wrote that he should receive a visit after the new year since the office would be closed during the holiday season. They wished him a Merry Christmas and a healthy, happy New Year. Henry was touched by their good wishes.

Henry got the news that Dorothy would be on his visitor list. Harry told him that Dorothy would be coming with Helen. Henry said they should try to sit near each other during the visit in case Dorothy felt a bit uncomfortable. Henry was looking forward to his first visitor. He hoped he didn't bombard Dorothy with too many questions about the manor, but he thought he should play it by ear until he senses that she was feeling comfortable. He didn't want her to wish she hadn't agreed to visit. After all, they have a lot of time.

DS Dunes was able to read the director's report on Henry's behavior. Since the start of his incarceration, Henry was unfriendly, uncooperative, and preferred to be alone. The report stated that after about six weeks, Henry's attitude changed. He was friendlier to staff and was to converse with other patients, especially one Harry Stratton. The director was a bit unsure of how that relationship would affect Henry's progress since he knew that Harry was an individual with a volatile nature. He advised the attendants to keep a closer watch when Henry and Harry were together. But he was surprised by Henry's change, especially after his first-day trip.

CHAPTER 19

Jr. had barely parked the car before Gina's parents were out the door. They had been waiting for what seemed like ages. You would think that they hadn't seen Gina for much longer than three months ago. So many hugs and kisses. Even Jr. got a hug from Gina's mother.

"Now mother," spoke up Mr. Locke. "Let Gina breathe; she will be here for two weeks." "I know," whispered Mrs. Locke. "Come in, come in," she added. "Father, help Jr. with the bags, please." "I have tea ready in the morning room," she added. "The sun is shining, and the birds are chirping. I think it will be the perfect place for tea. Don't you think, Gina?" she asked. "The morning room will be just the thing, mom. I hope you didn't go to too much bother for us," replied Gina. "Don't get me started," mentioned her dad. "Your mother had me doing this and that and then double-checking what I did, and you know your mother," he added.

Gina exclaimed, "it's perfect, mom," as they walked into the morning room. "What do you think, Jr.?" "As you said, this is just perfect, and look at all that good food," mumbled Jr. "Come on, mother," added Mr. Locke, "the kids must be hungry."

After a pleasant lunch, Gina asked her mother to help her unpack. When they got to her room, Gina told her mother that she and Jr. are officially dating. "I really like him, mom," gushed Gina. "He is such a gentleman, and when he takes me around to see some of the historical sites, and the way he explains them, it makes them almost feel real. He attends church with us, and then we all go to Arthur's grandmothers for lunch." "I'm so glad you're happy," replied her mom. "I must say you are glowing. But don't rush into anything, and don't let anything interfere with your studies." "I won't, mom," assured Gina. "My education is the most important thing in my life at the moment. I want to learn as much as I can about estate managing so Arthur and I can make this manor prosper. And I also want to receive my Arts certificate. I will draw and paint in my spare time and hope I can sell some of my work. And, you and dad are also very important to me, as well as Jr. When we are home for the summer, Arthur and I plan to have regular meetings about what we are doing and what we hope to accomplish for the manor. We will be coming to you and dad for your advice and opinions. The manor will be our home first, and then we will work it progressively into a successful business."

"Let's go downstairs, dad wanted to go for a walk around the grounds," added her mom. "He had some suggestions about some work he thinks could be done, and he would like to get your opinion, and Jr.'s opinion as well. He will show it to Arthur when he gets here next week. By the way, what do you think of Christine? Her parents seemed like nice people; we had a good talk on the phone." "I found Christine to be a very kind and understanding person. I feel like I've known her forever. I'm glad Arthur has met her. He seems so grown up now; it must be the idea of having so much responsibility on his shoulders. I feel he will make a great partner to share in the ownership of the manor," added Gina. "Sometimes, even I find myself wondering if all this is not a dream. Since I've lived here all my life, it's hard to think that we will be involved in making changes I love this place."

"You do know that Jr.'s firm is in charge of the estate's finances?" Mrs. Locke added. "He will need to be informed of any major changes and what the costs will be. He cannot refuse you the money for your proposed changes since you and Arthur are of age, but Jr. can offer advice. Also, your father and I are always available to impart any knowledge we have gained during our many years living here." "I know, mom, Jr. has already mentioned briefly what his firm's role is. Arthur and I do not think we can manage this manor on our own; we will certainly appreciate any advice you and dad can offer," stated Gina.

"It's good to be home," sighed Gina, as she bounced on her bed. "My room smells so fresh, mom, "she added. "I bet you washed all bedding and the drapes, and I thank you." "Nothing is too good for my daughter," pointed out her mom. "I'm sure your bed on campus is comfortable, but I bet you miss your bed." "Which room have you prepared for Jr.?" asked Gina. "It's the front room in the east wing," added her mom. "I hope he will be comfortable." "I'm sure he will be fine; after all, he is only here for two nights," puts in Gina. "And, which rooms do you have ready for Arthur and Christine?" inquired Gina. "I have the room just down the hall from yours for Christine," pointed out her mom, "Do you think she will like it? And for Arthur, I'll put him in the room down the hall from Jr.'s room in the east wing." "Thanks so much, mom," mentioned Gina. "I know everyone will appreciate all the hard work you and dad did for our visit. You are the best parents a girl can have."

After unpacking her few items, Gina went out and wandered around the manor grounds. She looked over the plot of land, where she planned to have the larger garden planted. It looked like her father had tilled it, and now it's ready for seeds. She can hardly wait for planting time. She brought her notebook out with her and sat down to make a drawing of where individual seeds were to be planted. She will be able to come home weekends to help her mother and Trisha (the girl from Cockernhoe) who had helped Mrs. Locke a few times previously and who had been promised that if she was available that she would be welcome to help when planting starts. Thinking of the plans they have for the future running of the manor is so exciting, Gina said to herself. I hope the months fly by.

CHAPTER 20

S ince George knew where Gina lives, he decided to send her an "I miss you" card, which he would not sign. He just couldn't wait until classes resume so he can be in closer contact with her. She won't need to know the card was from him at this time. He decided he would call Eloise and ask her if she would like to go for tea.

"Hi, Eloise, I was wondering if you would like to go for tea tomorrow," asked George. "Who is this?" demanded Eloise. "It's me, George, from college," he states. "How did you get my number?" Eloise asked. "I got it from one of your classmates; I told her I was going to pick you up on our way to study group, but I couldn't make it and that I didn't want you to be waiting alone in the dark." He added. "Don't get mad at her; she was concerned about your safety." "But we never planned to go to a study group together at all, why did you lie?" Eloise demanded. "I'm sorry, I was under the impression that we had made such a plan, I apologize." "Forget it," puts in Eloise. "I have to go. Please don't call me again." "Why?" demanded George. "I would like to take you to tea as an apology." "No, thank you," added Eloise. "I have to go. Goodbye."

After Eloise hung up, George sat fuming; he was quite upset. How dare she treat him like that, like someone lower than she is. Nobody treats me like that and gets away with it. George comforts himself, making a plan for what he was going to do next. He would like to make friends with Eloise only because she is such a good friend of Gina's. He remembered that Arthur and Christine were still in London. Maybe he will call them and invite them out. He just has to remember Arthur's grandmother's name. Once they meet, George will show interest in Arthur's background and Christine's. He thinks if Arthur likes him, then he could become one of them. Then he feels he could find out more about Gina from Arthur since they both are from Cockernhoe.

CHAPTER 21

It's visiting day, and Henry was more nervous than he let on. He didn't want anything to go wrong. He had a shower and shave. He even applied some aftershave lotion, but only a little, he doesn't want to offend anyone. When he walked into the visiting area, Henry felt a little flutter in his stomaChapter You would think this is my first date, the way I feel; he chides himself. Relax, take a deep breath, he reminded himself. He would not have recognized Dorothy if he didn't see Harry sitting with them. She's prettier than he remembered. It has been a very long time since he had last seen her. Henry slowly and nervously approached the table. Dorothy thinks that he looks about the same, but older. She was also nervous about this visit since she doesn't know why he would want her to visit him. Helen told her that Henry had no one else to visit him, and Harry felt sorry for his friend.

"I am so happy that you took the time to visit me," Henry said to Dorothy as soon as he sat down. "No problem, but I must admit I am curious as to why you wanted me to visit," she stated. "It's just that growing up I didn't make many friends, here or even at college. There were a couple of fellas in college that I hung out with a bit after our soccer games, but none I would consider a close friend. Even in the forces, I was too busy being scared and trying to stay alive that I didn't want to get too close to any of the others. We all just wanted to survive," added Henry. "But why me," questioned

Dorothy? "Since we are both from Cockernhoe, and because I have no family, I would like to get news from outside from someone I know. It's not the same as hearing it second hand or on the radio," stated Henry. "I will understand if, after today, that you do not wish to visit again. We didn't know each other well at all when we were younger, and since I am about ten years your senior, we didn't have the same interests or friends. If you do decide not to visit anymore, maybe you could be my pen pal. What do you think? No need to say so now, please think about it," he added.

CHAPTER 22

Gina was enjoying her time at home. She and her mom have been seen together with notebooks wandering around the manor grounds. Gina especially would like to have a plan in mind for the garden before she went back to London, but she knew it was too early in the season for planting. Her list of what she wants to plant is long, so with her mom's experience, they are drawing up the plan as to what is to be planted where. Her mom suggested that Gina keep a journal of all ideas, whether carried out or not. Her father teased them, saying that Gina is a chip off the old block. Her mother was always that way, having a plan, and being impatient to have it carried out. Even with Gina's inexperience, she realized the truth in that, but it doesn't stop her from dreaming of the finished garden.

During a break in their planning, the mail was delivered. There was something for Gina. She was curious as to whom it was from, since there was no return address, excepting that it was from London. Upon opening it, Gina gasped. "What is it," asked her mom. "Is everything alright?" "I'm not sure," replied Gina. "It's not signed, and it says, "I miss you. I have no idea who it could be from." "Could it be from your friend, Eloise," asked her mom. "I don't think so, and I'm sure she would sign her name. Is it okay if I call her?" "Go ahead, my dear," replied her mom. "You'll let me know what she says, won't you?" "Yes, I will," stated Gina. "I'll be right back," she added as she went into the house.

"Hi Eloise, it's Gina, how are you?" "I'm just fine; this is a pleasant surprise. How are you?" asked Eloise. "It's good to hear your voice," added Gina. "How are things in London?" "Well," replied Eloise. "My brother and sister go back to school on Monday, and my cousins will be here Saturday so that we will have a full house this weekend. How are your parents?" "They're fine, happy that I'm home, even if it is just for two weeks. By the way, thanks for the card," mentioned Gina. "What card?" questioned Eloise. "The one I got today in the mail. It says, "I miss you. I just assumed it was from you. It didn't have a return address, but the postmark shows it is from London. Didn't you send it?" queried Gina. "No, it wasn't me," added Eloise. "Sorry. Who do you think it was from?" "I'm not sure. This is strange, don't you think?" added Gina. "Could it be from one of your other classmates that you gave your address to, and don't remember you did so?" stated Eloise. "No, I'm very sure I didn't give anyone my address, did I give it to you?" questioned Gina. "Not your house address, but I know the name of the town. Maybe one of the others also remembered the name of your town. I guess you will have to wait until you get back to college and ask around." added Eloise. "I guess so," stated Gina. "I will have to forget about it until then. Thanks, Eloise." "Oddly, you should mention something strange happening," stated Eloise. "I had a strange phone call." "Who was it from?" inquired Gina. "It was George, and he asked to take me to tea. It weirded me out. I told him I'm too busy and not to call again. Now, every time the phone rings, I think it might be him. What do you think I should do if he does call again?" asked Eloise. "Maybe you can ask your family that if a guy phones to take a message and you will call back. That way, they screen your calls," added Gina. "What if my parents ask questions? What should I tell them?" wondered Eloise. "Tell them it's a guy from college that you're not sure you like him enough to go out with and will tell him that, when you return his message, that is if he does call again," decided Gina. "How did he get your number?" "He said he asked one of my classmates, using the excuse that we were part of the study group and that he had forgotten my number. He didn't tell me her name. I must go, mom is calling. See you in about ten days. Enjoy your visit with your parents and say hi to Jr.," added Eloise. "Bye." "Bye," added Gina.

Gina went out to the terrace with a thoughtful look. "Was it Eloise who sent the card," her mom asked. "No," stated Gina. "I guess it will be a mystery." "Never mind," puts in her mom, "Come help me make dinner. Your dad and Jr. must be getting hungry."

After dinner Jr. and Gina went for a long walk since he has to go back to work tomorrow, Gina will miss him, but she has so many thoughts crowding her mind that she will feel that she won't be ignoring Jr... She felt like a child at Christmas, wondering which present to open first. She plans to go through all seventeen rooms, some that had been closed off for lack of use to check if anything needed repairing. She knew that the nursery and the upstairs servant's quarters won't be in use for a while, but they will all get a good cleaning. Her mom will hire Trisha to come and help with that chore. Only the rooms that are in use will be repainted or papered. The window cleaning can wait until she is home for the summer, so her mother doesn't have too much to do, even though Trisha could be very helpful. Her mother agreed with her plans and will be happy to wait until summer to work with her daughter.

Arthur and Christine are due in a few days, so they must prepare their rooms first.

CHAPTER 23

Dorothy's first visit with Henry was over and as she and Helen were on the bus going home, she confessed that she was scared of being around murderers and suChapter Helen reminded her that she was visiting a murderer. "I know that," added Dorothy, "but he was such a nice guy, he didn't seem like a murderer." "What should murderers seem like?" asked Helen. "I'm not sure, maybe gruff-looking, with scary eyes. I don't know," confessed Dorothy. "Henry was not at all like that. It's hard to believe that he murdered three people." "Did he say anything to you about their plans?" asked Helen. "No, he thought I should get to know him first before agreeing to help in any way. He wants me to write to him, which I will do," added Dorothy. "How is Harry doing? He looked happy enough." "His moods come and go, that's one of the reasons he's in there. As long as he keeps up with his meds and continues therapy, he's okay. But he's the type that once he feels okay, then he figures he can quit taking the meds. Then here we go. He has been cautioned about that in the past but doesn't always listen. I'm trying to remind him not to quit his meds so his behavior won't change, and when it does, the attendants are constantly watching him, which makes him mad. It's a vicious circle. He is trying because he desperately wants out of there," stated Helen.

"Are you able to go next week?" asked Helen. "I can't," added Dorothy. "I have a school field trip I volunteered to help chaperone.

I told Henry I would write to him. He cautioned me not to mention anything other than everyday stuff. What about you, are you going next week?" "No, I can't either. My boys have dentist appointments. It wouldn't hurt the guys not to have visitors next week. When they do see us, we will have more to tell them," added Helen.

It's the second time visiting Henry, and Dorothy felt much more relaxed. Henry was telling her what his plans were. On the next day trip, which will be to Covent Gardens, there will be street performers and a lot of people, so it should be easy to sneak away. Then they will take the tube farther down the line, and then steal a car. They will drive to Luton, where they will abandon it and walk the rest of the way to the crofter's cottage. It will be dark by then, so they won't be too noticeable. Henry asked that they please fill the cottage with enough food so that they won't have to take the chance of raising suspicion with all their coming and going. After all, the police will be watching Helen because she is Harry's sister. And since Dorothy visited him, Henry is also sure the police will be watching her.

Harry is also saying similar things to Helen. They must be cautious when going out to the cottage. They shouldn't come out to the cottage if the police are still around Rumforton. "Try to act normal," Henry encouraged them.

CHAPTER 24

The two weeks were coming to an end, and soon it would be time to go back to college. After Arthur and Christine arrived at the manor, they spent a few days showing her the sights. They walked to Cockernhoe, where Arthur showed them his home that his mother boarded up until he decides what he wants to do with it. He will seek advice from Mr. Locke and Jr. about renting it versus selling it. While Arthur and Christine were wandering around, Gina met with Trisha. They may have met in the past, but since Gina is four years older than Trisha, she would have been attending the school for more former students, whereas Trisha was attending the school for lower-level students. Gina felt comfortable with Trisha and thought that she would be an excellent help to her mother while she was away at college. They would start planting the following weekend. Arthur, Christine, and Gina would come home for that. Arthur would be working with Mr. Locke planning their day, while Gina, Christine, and Trisha would be helping Mrs. Locke with the planting. As some artists say, they could see the finished product, but getting there is part of the challenge.

Jr. would drive down for a day, and then he would drive Gina, Arthur and Christine back to London. He had missed Gina, but they talked to each other every night. He told his parents that he planned to take two weeks off during the summer break, so he can spend that time at the manor helping Arthur and Mr. Locke with some of the proposed changes such as adding a small pond with goldfish and water lilies.

The day had arrived, and there were tears shed. "It's only for a week," Mr. Locke reminded his wife. "I know, I know," she replied. "It was good to have Gina and the others here, and summer break is only about three months away. Arthur said he and Christine would stay in London for the first week then come to the manor. Christine can only stay a week here before going home to Kirkcudbright."

"Do you have the list of the seeds that we are going to start planting next weekend?" Margaret asked Morris. "Yes, dear," he replied. "I have both lists, the one from Gina and the one from Arthur. I will go into Luton tomorrow and pick up everything I can there; if not, then I will have to go to London." "And I am going to plan my menu for this coming weekend. I don't want to spend too much time cooking; I will want to spend a lot of time helping with the planting. Here is my list of things I need," added Mrs. Locke as she handed her husband her rather long list. As he was leaving the kitchen to go out into the yard and check if anything is missing on his list, Mr. Locke heard his wife humming to herself, something she hasn't done in a long time. He said to himself; I'm glad she's happy.

CHAPTER 25

Not only was Mrs. Locke counting the days when Gina and Arthur will be back for the weekend, but George was also counting the days when classes will resume, then he would see Gina again. This past week he had wanted to call Eloise again, but the way she sounded on the first call, had him decide not to chance to get her upset enough that she would tell her parents that he may be stalking her, which he isn't but given his past, the police may not believe him. It's wasn't his fault; she fell down the stairs at the tube station and now has limited use of her legs and has to be in a wheelchair. He can wait, he told himself, just a few more days. His impatience was one thing that got him caught at the last college. Should I send another "I miss you card" to Gina, he wondered. Better not, remember I must be patient, he reminded himself.

Eloise and Gina have both forgotten about the way George made them feel creeped out. He didn't realize that they felt that way about him. Why must things be so difficult, he asked himself. I like Gina and would like to get to know her better. What is so wrong with that? But, if he were, to be honest with himself, he would remember what the psychologist told him and his parents about what happened at the other college. Anyway, what do they know; he thought to himself.

Jr. drove into the college parking lot to allow the others to remove their bags from the boot of his car. George just happened to be walking through the parking lot at that time and felt it was fate that brought him there. "Hello, everyone," he called. "What a pleasant surprise. Here, let me help you," he offered, as he went to pick up Gina's bag. "No thanks," stated Gina, "Jr. can take it for me." "How was your break?" he asked. "It sure was quiet around here." "It was relaxing as well as productive," puts in Arthur. "Sorry to rush everyone," announced Jr., "but we have dinner arrangements, remember." "Good night, George," puts in Arthur. "See you in class." George is fuming as he watches Jr. and Gina drive away. That damn Arthur, he says.

It was back to the books again. During free time, students were asking each other how their break was. There was a seriousness in the atmosphere. The students were putting more energy into the last three months of class. They wanted to go for summer holidays with high marks. Gina and Jr. had discussed her schedule, and they decided that they would only see each other once or twice during the week, but try to talk each night. They would still attend church and go to Arthur's mother's for lunch, and then when he drove them back to the college, he and Gina would spend some time alone before saying goodnight. Arthur and Christine did the same thing. It was easier for them because they were able to see each other between classes. Eloise and Gina's friendship seemed to become stronger. They walked to class together and met for lunch, then walked back to the dorms after class. They would even meet at the library after dinner to study together. George witnessed the amount of time they spent together and was feeling possessive of Gina. He thought he must do something about it. One time he had another student tell Eloise that she had a phone call, which gave George some time to watch Gina. He was about to approach her when Eloise came back. "What's wrong," Gina asked her? "You looked confused." "I am," sconfessed Eloise. Penny came and told me I had a phone call, but when I got there, there was no one on the line. I asked Penny who it was, and she said she didn't know. She told me that George told her there was a call for me, now why would he do that?" "Oh, creepy George, what could he be up to," asked Gina. "I don't know, but it still gives me the willies when I think of him peering at us." "Let's get this section done; I want to get back in time to get Jr.'s call," added Gina.

It has been three weeks since classes resumed. George managed to figure out Gina's schedule. Her classes coincided with Eloise's, so they walk together; except Thursday evenings. Gina had a class in Hall B, while Eloise had one in Hall C. Since Gina's class ended at 9:30 and Eloise's at 9 p.m., Gina would have to walk back to her dorm alone. This Thursday, George was waiting along the path to Gina's dorm and startled her as she was walking by the fountain. "Hi, Gina," he called. "How are you? Are you going back to the dorms? I can walk with you." "No, thanks," said Gina. "I have something I'm thinking about and just need to walk alone." "No problem," added George. "I can just walk with you to make sure you're safe." "There's no need for you to do that, with all these other students around," pointed out Gina, "But thanks anyway, goodnight. There's Arthur and Christine." "Hi, Gina," called Arthur. "We were just going for a walk, and Christine mentioned that you have a class here, so we thought we would walk this way and walk you to your dorm." "Thanks so much," added Gina. "Goodnight, George."

"Thanks for saving me," mentioned Gina. "George was insisting he should walk with me to keep me safe, and I only wanted to be safe from him. He is so creepy." "I think I should talk with him soon," added Arthur. "I think that's a great idea," pointed out Christine. I remember you and Eloise telling me he made you feel creepy. What is Eloise doing tonight?" "She has a class in Hall C, but Mike will walk her home. You remember Mike, don't you," questioned Gina. "He's the blond guy from the United States. I see them talking quite a lot." "I didn't realize that Eloise was sweet on someone," mentioned Christine. "I've had the opportunity to talk to him a few times, he seems like such a nice guy, and I love his accent."

CHAPTER 26

The day trip Henry and Harry had their hearts set on was postponed due to an outbreak of the flu at the hospital. Henry was permitted to make a phone call to Dorothy, advising her that she could not visit the following week because of the postponement. It was for the better since it would give the ladies more time to provision the cottage. Helen and Dorothy felt the waiting to be very stressful.

On their next visit to the hospital, Helen and Dorothy found out that the day trip had been scheduled for late-August. Henry said it gave them more time to prepare and for him to double-check his plans. Dorothy told Henry how happy Mrs. Locke was that her daughter, Trisha, is so helpful and that she would be working there over the summer helping Mrs. Locke and Gina with the garden. Gina had planned for it to be much bigger, and Trisha liked working with Gina and her mother. Trisha also told her mom that Arthur had plans to build or repair one of the outbuildings for a chicken coop. "It seems like the Lockes are fixing things up at the manor," added Henry. "Have you heard anything about who is in charge of things at the manor?" "No," said Dorothy, "It seemed like they have been living quietly since Gina and Arthur were away at college. They come home some weekends and during breaks. They have about three months until summer break. I am glad that Trisha will be working there. It's good for her to make money and learn from Mrs.

Locke. I like the Lockes, they are such kind people." "How is Harry taking the delay in your plans?" she asked. "Of course he wasn't pleased, but what can I do? Things happen," added Henry. "But it took a while for me to calm him down enough to listen to me. It wouldn't do for him to have a fit at this point." "He seems pretty relaxed now," pointed out Dorothy. "He does enjoy it when Helen visits." "Are you sure you want to do this for us, for me?" Henry asked. "You can walk away from it since you hardly know me. I know it's probably not easy for you. You have no idea how much I appreciate it."

"Yes, I must admit I am finding it stressful, but I would like to help," stated Dorothy. "I heard that you were sent to Bethlehem Royal Hospital because you have a psychological problem. I feel that someone with issues like you have, should not be held responsible for their actions. I guess it's better that you are in Bethlehem Royal hospital than in another prison. You would receive better treatment for your issues, and when they feel you have them under control, maybe you could be released sooner than if you were in another prison. So, can I ask, why did you murder the Beavingtons? What have they ever done to you?" whispered Dorothy. "I would rather not talk about it right now, stated Henry. "Please forgive me for asking, but it's for my peace of mind," she added. "And I have to consider my children. If the police found out I helped, I would go to goal and who would look after them? My husband had left us, and I don't think he would want to look after them, even though they are also his. I do have a sister in London, and she could probably take them in. She and her husband did not have children, and she loves her niece and nephews." "Please, try not to worry," added Henry. "I am sure the police will stop looking for us after a while; if they think we left England. I still have to finalize that part of my plan. I will let you know what I've decided well before the day of the day trip. But, you can still walk away from it. I am not holding you to anything. Helen would be able to do it on her own."

CHAPTER 27

"So how are you and Jr. getting along?" asked Eloise. "Have you met his parents yet? I know you have only been dating for about nine months, but do you think he may be the one? He seemed so attentive to you, and I know you think the world of him." "Yes," added Gina, "it has only been nine months, and I do care for him a lot, but he is only my first boyfriend, so if it's meant to be, then so be it, but I am in no hurry for marriage. After all, I still have one more year of college, and I am only 18 years old — lots of time."

"So what course is Mike taking, and what are his plans for the future? Would he go home or stay in London and look for a job?" questioned Gina. "He's taking sciences because he wants to be a small animal veterinarian. He had not told me any specific plans for the future, and it's too early in our relationship to expect him to stay in London just for me. I will see how things progress. Now, let's get studying." "I insist we keep each other informed of the progress of our relationships," added Eloise. "Oh, and how are Arthur and Christine doing? They seem right for each other. What do you think?" "Yes, I do agree with you, they seem to belong together, but neither has said what will happen when Christine has finished her second year here in London. What course is she taking anyway?"

"She's taking general journalism and may specialize at a later date," mentioned Gina. "So much for distractions, let's get studying."

Again neither of them noticed George peering through the café window. He realized that in a few short weeks, it will be summer break, and he would not be seeing Gina for two months. That thought does not please him. He was so busy grumbling to himself that he doesn't notice Arthur outside the bookstore across the street. After he watched George watch Gina and Eloise, Arthur decided that he must do something about it. He realized that George was up to something concerning Gina and Eloise and thinks that maybe he should talk to Jr. He called Jr. and asked if they could meet tomorrow evening at a café about four blocks from the college, so there would be no chance either Gina, Eloise, or Christine see them.

"What is this all about?" Jr. asked Arthur. "It sounded serious, is everyone alright?" "It concerns Gina and Eloise. There is a student in some of their classes whom the girls think is stalking them. They told me he gives them the creeps. At first, I thought it would be natural he is in the area they are because he is a classmate, but last night I noticed him peering in the window of the café where they were talking. He was hiding behind a bush. That was why I decided to talk to you, and we can figure out what to do about it." "What is the guy's name?" asked Jr. "It's George," added Arthur. "Do you mean the guy who wanted to help Gina with her luggage when we came back from Cockernhoe?" "Yes, that's him," added Arthur. "He seemed okay, but I don't want to dismiss what the girls told me. What do you think we should do?"

CHAPTER 28

There was so much of the flu going around at the hospital that Henry knew there will be no day trips for a while. Henry believed it's for the better because he has been rethinking his plans. He decided that they would steal a car, drive to an area close to the crofter's cottage where Helen and Dorothy will have left clothes, money, and some food. Then they would drive to Dover and take the ferry to Calais and hide in that city for at least six months, or until Helen or Dorothy let them know that the police have not been around so muChapter

After Henry read the notice informing the residents that the same persons who were on the list to go to the Covent Gardens will be the ones who will go on the next day trip, which would be mid-December, he decided that their escape attempt will be then. He thought that it would give the ladies more time to get everything ready, especially the money. Henry and Harry do have some cash with them, but it won't be enough to survive until they find part-time jobs, which is one of the first things they would need to do when they arrive in Calais. The only downfall to their plans is the issue of their medications. They will have to make do without until they're settled in Calais and go to a free clinic.

The director of the hospital would allow each resident one phone call per week to replace the fact that there can be no visits. The health board suggested that no letters are to be mailed, but the residents can receive letters from family and friends. The hospital had never seen such an outbreak as this one in many years. There were even a few deaths, and because of that, the director was rigorous on daily cleanings. The residents were grumbling all about it, but the director continued to tell them it is for their good. And even some of the attendants were becoming grumpy. Before they could leave for home, they were required to go through a strict process to decontaminate themselves. They also had to go through the same regime when arriving for work. It was inconvenient but necessary.

Knowing Henry's plan to live in Calais until the police decide that the escapees are not in Rumforton or Cockernhoe, Helen thought it would be a good idea to get a pen pal from Calais. So when Harry wrote to her, it wouldn't look suspicious that she would be receiving letters with a French postmark. The pen pal she found was a woman about her age, also a single mother. The language barrier would not be a problem because Helen knew some French, and the lady in Calais knew some English. The lady's name was Clementine. She has twin boys named Francois and Giles. She would tell Harry on her next visit, once the quarantine has been lifted at the hospital or maybe she'll write to him about it.

CHAPTER 29

“I suggest we go about it in a very casual manner. We don't want George to get angry; after all, we don't know that much about him. We can't know what he might do if angered." stated Jr. "I have to think about this like the solicitor I am; we don't want charges brought against us. How about we just happen to meet up with him and sort of befriend him. Then take it from there. What do you think?" "Sounds good to me," added Arthur. "I can find out his schedule for when he will be alone some evening after class. I suggest we don't say anything to the girls, for now, anyway," he added.

Meanwhile, George was in his dorm room, thinking about Gina and how he could spend some time with her before the summer break, and somehow finding out her address and phone number at the manor. He does not want to imagine that he won't be able to see or even talk to her for two whole months. "I must think of something," he said to himself. "She is meant to be with me, not Jr. I don't have the money that he does, but I can still make her happy."

Little do the girls know that Arthur and Jr are discussing them. They are studying together with Christine in Gina's dorm room. Here they feel that George cannot be peering at them, or that he cannot be in their dorm building since it is a female dorm only. They would prefer to study in the library or at the local café.

"What plans do you have for the summer?" Gina asked Christine and Eloise. "My parents will be coming to London for a week so they can meet Arthur's mother and grandmother, then we will go on a road trip on our way home," said Christine. "I will come back to London two weeks before classes resume when Arthur picks me up, and we will spend those two weeks at the manor. I am looking forward to it. Again, thank you for the invitation." She turned to Eloise. "How about you, Eloise?" "For the first two weeks, I will stay in London. Mike has a part-time job in London which I like. The following week is when I will be able to go to the manor, and again, thanks for the invitation, Gina. For the rest of the summer, I will stay in London, since I also have a part-time job. Mike and I will be able to see each other when our schedules allow." stated Eloise. "I am so glad that your parents allow you to invite friends home." "Yes, they are wonderful parents, but if you think about it, they see another person as extra help. They only have to feed you and provide a bed. Mom always said it's like the old days when more people were living at the manor," added Gina. "Let's go for a walk after we've finished studying, I don't think I will be able to sleep with so much going on in my head," mentioned Christine.

Luck must be on his side, thinks George. He decided to go for a walk to clear his head and who does he see, but Gina, Eloise, and Christine, also going for a walk. He followed them. If anyone asked, he would tell them that he was following them to make sure they are safe since it is quite late. It would have been a perfect ending to a frustrating day if Gina was out walking alone, but he thinks that Gina would never walk alone this late. He was sure that her parents have advised her about the foolishness of walking alone late at night. George is so engrossed in his thoughts about Gina that he doesn't notice Arthur following him. This instance decided Arthur that he and Jr. would have to have their "talk" with George sooner rather than later.

The girls have just now entered their dorm, so George turned to go back to his dorm. Arthur had to quickly hide behind a tall bush so George wouldn't see him. Arthur followed George and saw that he was going back to their dorm and waited for a few minutes before entering the building.

CHAPTER 30

Helen told Dorothy that she got a letter from her pen pal. "Why did you decide to get a pen pal?" asked Dorothy. "My mother sent me an advertisement about it awhile ago, and I just put it away. I thought I had lost it, but when I was cleaning up my desk, I found it and decided to go ahead with it," stated Helen. "How does it work?" asked Dorothy. "You fill out a form stating your preferences, i.e., female, approximate age, etc. and they match you up," added Helen. "I thought it would be a good idea to get one from Calais since the guys will be living there for a while and they can write me, and there won't be any suspicion when I get a letter with a French postmark because I will have been receiving letters from there already." "I think that was a great idea," added Dorothy. Maybe I should apply for one. It wouldn't hurt, and it's not just for the guys, but it will be someone to talk to and confide in. We do have each other, but with someone from another country, it would be interesting." "I'll bring the information with me next time I come to visit," stated Helen. "I wrote to Harry about it awhile ago. I remember when we were young, one of our teachers mentioned that, but our mom didn't think it was a good idea. I guess she's had a change of mind."

"How are we going to get money to set aside for the guys?" asked Dorothy. "Since Harry has been in hospital, I am in charge of his finances. He doesn't need much money for anything, but I will withdraw small amounts from time to time so as not to raise suspicion. I am using the money for my travel expenses to visit him. As for Henry, maybe the next time you visit him suggest that he arrange for you to receive monies for the reason that he wants someone near to check on his cottage and go in to do a bit of cleaning. It's a legitimate reason." added Helen. "I got a call from Harry this morning saying that the quarantine was lifted, and we can visit. I was thinking of going Friday, can you come also?" asked Helen. "That's good that they can receive visitors. I'm sure it has been hard for those who received regular visitors, like Henry and Harry. Yes, I can come with you Friday," Dorothy said.

During the visit, Henry told Dorothy that they would be going on the day trip two weeks from this Friday. Harry and Helen are at the same table visiting so they can all be together when discussing the final details. "Do you have everything ready?" he asked Dorothy. "Yes, we do," she added. "Remember, don't change your routine," added Henry. "Do you remember that Helen told you she now has a pen pal who lives in Calais?" added Dorothy. "I also have signed up for one, so if you write from Calais, no one should be suspicious. I will have let the postmistress know about my pen pal, so she will think it is only a letter from my pen pal."

CHAPTER 31

Arthur found out George's schedule and told Jr. that the upcoming Thursday evening would be a great time to "meet George" accidentally on purpose as he leaves the lab building. It would be close to 10 p.m., and there won't be too many other students out, except those who are in the building with George. Most of the students would be hurrying back to their dorms, given the lateness of the hour.

Jr. found out that as long as they don't explicitly say things like "you'll be sorry, or you better watch out," then it would look like they are just having a friendly conversation. Also, we should make sure there are no witnesses. They decided to meet at the rotunda at about 9:45 p.m.

"There he is," pointed out Jr. "Evening George," said Arthur. "Who are you?" George asked. "My name is Arthur, and this is Jr., do you remember us? I'm Christine's boyfriend, and Jr. is Gina's boyfriend. You met us when we returned to campus after the two-week break, and you offered to help Gina with her luggage." "Yes, I do remember," added George. "What can I do for you? Is Gina alright?" asked George with a hint of concern in his voice. "Gina and Christine are fine," added Jr. We wanted to talk to you about them and Eloise." "Why?" questioned George. "I haven't done anything wrong."

"As far as the girls, Arthur and I are concerned, you have," stated Jr. "Gina and Eloise have told us that they feel you are stalking them, and it gave them the creep when they see you lurking around. So if that is the case, we would suggest you stop. We do not want to have to go to the authorities." "Are you threatening me?" asked George. "No, we are not. We only suggest that you stop stalking the girls. If you're not doing anything wrong, then why are you getting defensive?" asked Jr. "I'm not getting defensive, and I resent the fact that Gina thought I would harm her. She was very kind to me on orientation day," added George.

"I have to get to my dorm. I have an early test tomorrow," stated George as he started to walk away." "Ok, but just make sure that we don't hear any more from the girls that they feel you are still stalking them. Do you understand?" stated Arthur. "Yes, yes, I understand," whispered George as he hurried away. "Well, how do you think that went?" Arthur asked Jr. "You can tell that he obviously is guilty about something. Did you notice that he couldn't look straight at us?" mentioned Jr.

"We'll tell the girls about our conversation with George on Sunday. Hopefully, they will get some comfort from it since they have to study for the final exams. They don't need any distractions, except from their boyfriends, of course," said Arthur. "I'll keep an eye on him also."

George was in his dorm room pacing; he is upset and mumbles about Jr. and Arthur's accusations. He is not stalking Gina. He only wanted to make sure she was okay. They obviously do not understand the role of a gentleman —, especially Jr., with his fancy car.

But for now, George decided he better study. Exams start Monday and continue for two weeks. He didn't want to fail any classes since his father told him he must pass with an acceptable mark since this was his last chance to get any further education. The tuition at the other college put a strain on his uncle's finances, and now with the added tuition for this college, his uncle wanted him to graduate and find a good job so he can become independent. I don't need Jr. and Arthur to add to the pressure, he said to himself. Damn them anyway.

Jr. and Arthur told the girls about their conversation with George. The girls promised they would watch out for George and tell Arthur or Jr. if they still felt he is stalking them. They said they didn't need this to be on their minds while they were studying.

Everyone at the college had exams on their mind. All students were studying even when they have free time until all hours of the night. They were concerned about getting high passing marks and excited that it'll all be over in two weeks.

CHAPTER 32

Gina's parents were also counting the days when she will be home. For two whole months, Mrs. Locke is beside herself. She hoped Gina has studied hard for the finals. They all want her to pass year one with a high grade. Mrs. Locke had a long list of what needs doing. She and Gina can go over it and prioritize it. The garden should be priority number one. Trisha had helped her with the planting and had come over once a week for weeding. Trish's brothers would go with her and help Mr. Locke with some outside chores. She had not seen her husband so happy now there are children around, even though it's only once a week.

Mr. & Mrs. Locke had driven over to Luton for supplies. It was closer than London, and if they did go to London, Mrs. Locke would want to go over to the college to see Gina. Her husband persuaded her not to, and they knew Gina needed to study and would also want to spend time with her classmate that she won't see for two months. She wanted to make Gina's favorite dinner, her first night home. They would have a relaxing evening, the four of them. Jr. would only stay the night; then, he had to return to London. He would drive down on the weekends until Gina's last two weeks in which time he would stay at the manor. That way, he can drive Gina back to college.

In the first two weeks, the Lockes would have Gina all to themselves, then Eloise would come to visit for one week. Arthur would drive her down, and then he would stay until just before he had to drive back to London and pick up Christine, who would be staying at the manor for two weeks before they all have to go back to college to begin their second year of studies. Jr. would drive Eloise back to London after her one week visit.

Exams were finally over, and everyone is excited about leaving. There were many goodbyes, and I'll miss you's being exchanged. George took that opportunity to wish Eloise and Christine a great summer holiday, but when he turned to Gina, after wishing her a great holiday, he whispered to her, "I'll miss you." She remembered the card she got over the spring break and what with the fact that George was stalking them, Gina realized that it must have been George who sent that card. She, Eloise, and Christine will be meeting with the guys in a short while, and Gina decided to tell them what George just said.

After Gina told Jr. and Arthur, they went directly to George's dorm room for a further conversation. "George, it's Arthur, are you there?" George didn't answer the door, but Arthur and Jr. knew he was there, they heard him mumbling. Arthur knocks again, this time harder. "George, open up, I know you're in there!" As George opens the door, a crack, Jr., and Arthur push it open and enter the room, and then they pushed the door closed. "You can't come in here," yelled George, with a tremor in his voice. "We certainly can, and we did," answered Jr. "We wanted to remind you about our conversation last week. Do you remember it?' "I haven't done anything," squeaked George. "Leave me alone; I have to pack." "Perhaps you didn't understand, we have one thing to say," added Arthur. "Do not stalk Gina, Eloise, or Christine ever again; as a matter of fact, do not even talk to them. Think about what we said over the summer break, and maybe change classes or even drop out. If you don't change classes, make sure to steer clear of the girls. If they ever notice you anywhere in their vicinity and tell us, we won't be so nice. You got that, George?" "All right, all right, I hear you," whispered George. "I will see about other classes; the counselor did say it wouldn't be too late for me to make a change. The course I want can be completed taking several alternative classes. Now, will you please leave." "Enjoy your summer break," stated Arthur with contempt.

Gina said her goodbyes to Eloise and Christine. They waited with her until Jr. drove up. By that time, Arthur came along. After loading her bags into Jr.'s car, there were hugs all around. Arthur drove Eloise home; he and Christine went to his grandmother's place.

The summer holidays had officially started.

CHAPTER 33

The long-awaited day had finally arrived. Henry's smile was like a boy who got the long-desired toy at Christmas. Even Harry had a smile on his lips. Henry had to caution him about not acting too excited. Someone may ask him why, even though it is only a day trip. Harry had never been on any of the day trips since he arrived there about five years ago. His excitement was genuine, but not for the day trip but for the fact he knows that he and Henry would be walking away from the group and their life at Bethlehem Royal Hospital. Harry wanted to jump and yell, yippee! Henry was staying close to him to keep him in line, but he understood Harry's mood. He also wanted to dance and shout yippee as the bus pulls up.

Six patients were going on this day trip. Two females and four males. There would be three attendants accompanying them; one was a female attendant.

As the bus was leaving the hospital grounds, Harry looked back with a look that said, "screw you." As they approached Covent Gardens, one of the attendants reminded the patients of the dos and don'ts. Do stay with the group, don't wander off. Do be courteous of the public, don't get pushy. Do this, do that, mumbled Harry. "Who do they think we are, grade school kids?" he asked Henry. "It's just the procedure they have to follow," added Henry. "Please don't do anything that would bring attention to yourself. We want to stay at the back of the group, so when it's time for us to leave, it would be easier. Do you understand that?"

"Yes, for sure," added Harry. "Freedom is so close; I can almost taste it." "Just be patient," warned Henry.

The itinerary was for the group to walk around the grounds and browse the open markets. After stopping to watch the street performers, they would continue onto the Phoenix Gardens and have a picnic lunChapter On the way back to the bus, they would stop for a tour of the London Transportation Museum, which housed vintage vehicles. If time permitted as they make their way back to the bus, they would be allowed to browse the other open markets in the immediate area.

During lunch, Harry was getting impatient. Henry had to remind him to relax. The plan was for Harry to pretend he was feeling sick to take the attention of at least one of the attendants. About that time, Henry would say he needed to use the men's room. What with all the commotion around Harry, the attendant just waved Henry towards the public washrooms. Then Harry would pretend he is going to throw up and started to hurry towards the restrooms as well. During all the confusion about Harry, the attendant watching the other males assumed that Henry had returned, so he told Harry to hurry.

As Harry got closer to the washrooms, Henry motioned him towards some tall bushes where he had hidden. Then they sprinted towards the Covent Garden tube station. Once they got on the train, Harry breathed a sigh of relief. "We are not in the clear yet," cautioned Henry. "We need to disembark at Chancery Lane station, where we will have to find a car to "borrow." Then we would be on our way to Rumforton. We should get there by dark and hope to get to the crofter's cottage where the ladies have packed what we will need. From the cottage, we need to drive to Dover, ditch the car and catch the ferry to Calais. Only then would I feel we are in the clear." stated Henry, confident that he had covered all bases.

Back at Covent Gardens, one of the attendants called the director to advise him that Henry and Harry were missing. The director suggested he remain in the garden and wait for the police to arrive and that the remaining four patients are to go back to the waiting bus. Once the police arrived, things happened very quickly. An APB was put out for Henry and Harry with a description of what they were wearing. After DS Dunes was informed, he called the manor to tell the Lockes the news. He advised them to keep an eye out and make sure all doors and windows are locked. He said to them that he is sending a Constable to the manor who would stay with them until he arrived. He didn't believe Henry would harm them, but they cannot be sure about Harry. The police don't know if they are together, maybe they went their separate ways. DS Dunes contacted the police department in Rumforton to give them a head's up. He suggested they speak with Helen and Dorothy in-person to provide them with the news. Face to face contact could prove beneficial in some cases, and this was one of those.

Both Helen and Dorothy had heard about the escape on the 6:00 o'clock news. Helen thought Dorothy would be getting nervous, so she called her to try to calm her and remind her to act surprised when the police ask if she knows where Henry was, she can honestly say no. Even Helen didn't know where they were. They would not be lying to the police, even though they have an idea of where they may be. Helen suggested to Dorothy that they should each have a cup of tea, and that Helen would call her tomorrow. They both decided to watch the 11 o'clock news for any further information.

All they heard was: "two men escaped from the Bethlehem Royal Hospital this afternoon. Do not approach them; they are dangerous. Call 999 if you see them. We will keep you informed of further developments."

PART II

CHAPTER 34

After Mr. Locke got off the phone with DS Dunes, he gathered everyone into the study to discuss the call. "DS Dunes just called to tell us that Henry had escaped from Bethlehem Hospital this afternoon. He doesn't believe Henry was dangerous, but we were to keep a lookout and lock all doors and windows at night. He was sending DC Rainey over to stay with us tonight until he can come himself tomorrow. He will be meeting with the director of the hospital this afternoon and will call us to inform us of any developments.

Meanwhile, he said not to worry and carry on as usual," stated Mr. Locke. "Are you sure, dear?" asked Mrs. Locke. "Yes, I am," replied Mr. Locke. "DS Dunes said that Henry confided to the director that he always liked us and wished us no harm. With all the therapy he has gone through and medications, he understands why he did what he did. According to the director and psychiatrist, they believe Henry had overcome that affliction." "He also mentioned that another man escaped with Henry, but he didn't know if they are together, that's why we must be vigilant. They have constables posted in Cockernhoe and Rumforton, where the other man is from," added Mr. Locke. "Oh, Mr. Locke, I'm so worried, we have a friend of Gina's coming next week for a week, and then Arthur and Christine will be here. What should we tell them?" asked Mrs. Locke. "We will need to explain to them and suggest they keep an eye out. Gina and Arthur knew what Mr. Chestermere looked like, so they will know not to approach him. We must make sure no-one is ever alone. Even though I believe that Henry would not do us any harm, we don't know anything about the other guy. As DS Dunes mentioned, we don't know if they are together or if they went their separate ways," added Mr. Locke.

Trisha had come to the manor for tea and to speak with Mrs. Locke and Gina about their plans. When Gina told her about the man who escaped from the Bethlehem Hospital, Trisha mentioned that he was the man her mother had been visiting. "I didn't realize that your mother knew Mr. Chestermere," said Mrs. Locke. "She didn't know him that well since he is about ten years older than she is. Her friend in Rumforton, who visits her brother at Bethlehem Hospital, felt sorry that Mr. Chestermere wasn't receiving any visitors, so mom agreed to visit him," added Trisha. "We must insist that when you leave here, someone will drive you home, even though DS Dunes told us that Mr. Chestermere always liked us, and doesn't mean us any harm, because there was the matter of the other escapee. They did not give us any information about him. Your mother would probably know more since she knows his sister. But we must always be vigilant," stated Mrs. Locke. "They are sending a constable here, and you will probably see more police around Cockernhoe since that's where Mr. Chestermere has his cottage. I'm also sure there will be more police around Rumforton." Trisha doesn't believe that her mother knows much about Helen's brother since she hasn't said anything to her. She vows to ask her mother when she gets home.

"After tea, we will go out to the garden to show Gina what we have accomplished thus far, and will go over the arrangements we have made for further changes," added Mrs. Locke. "Mr. Locke and Jr. will go out and look at what the plans are for moving ahead when Arthur comes home. The main thing is that we carry on, as usual, no matter the news about Mr. Chestermere escaping and keeping an eye out in case he came back here."

CHAPTER 35

Henry and Harry got to the outskirts of Rumforton just after dark. Harry wanted to see his sister, but Henry told him that would be foolish. "Let's just get to the crofter's cottage, grab the stuff, and drive over to Dover and catch the ferry. The farther away I am from England, the better I'll feel," said Henry. "Are you sure you remember the way?" he asked Harry. "You must remember I haven't been here in over five years," added Harry. "Give me a minute to orientate myself. Things have overgrown so muChapter There's the path, let's go." "We will change clothes here but take them with us and ditch them when we ditch the car," mentioned Henry. "Let's go." "It's sure good to be out of Bethlehem, isn't it," added Harry.

The drive to Dover didn't take long, and before they knew it, Henry and Harry were relaxing on the ferry as it pulled away from the dock. "Not too much longer, and we'll be in France," stated Henry. "Let's go for a snack."

"What should we do when we get there?" queried Harry. "We'll stay in a hostel until we find jobs. We won't contact anyone at home for a while," stated Henry. "The police will be watching them closely, I'm sure. It really was a great idea Helen had to get a pen-pal so it wouldn't look suspicious when she receives our letters from France. Dorothy also got one. It will be hard on them for a while, but they can both honestly say they do not know where we were since I just told Dorothy we would catch the ferry and head out from there. I didn't tell her we would be staying in Calais." "Just seeing the stars and feeling the light breeze is heaven," mentioned Harry. "I never want to ever end up in a place like Bethlehem again." "Yes, you must admit it is a wonderful feeling to be free," added Henry. "Was Helen able to find that French dictionary?" Henry asked.

"For sure, I have it here in my bag," remarked Harry. "Once we get settled, we can have a look at it before we go out to buy dinner," added Henry. While they were out for dinner, Henry picked up a local newspaper to look for jobs. "We might as well get started with the job hunt," he told Harry. There seems to be quite a desire for manual laborers. I'm sure we will be working before the week is over." "When can I write Helen?" asked Harry. "I think we should wait at least a month to give some time for things to cool down. Once the police are satisfied that we are not in the Cockernhoe or Rumforton area, they will start to search further out. They may even think we were hiding somewhere in London since it's such a big city. I will keep my eyes on the newspapers for further developments." stated Henry.

CHAPTER 36

Mrs. Locke was finding it hard to carry on as usual. Even though she liked Mr. Chestermere, and DS Dunes said he regretted what he did, she cannot forget it. She didn't want to scare Gina or Trisha, so she tried to immerse herself into the plans she and Gina discussed during the spring break. Now that the garden was growing, the ladies will start on the ideas for the upstairs rooms. Gina wanted to start with the nursery, but her mom had to make an excuse to wait awhile. During the spring break, Arthur had asked her and Mr. Locke their opinion about building a studio for Gina, and the nursery seemed like the perfect place. It had several windows letting in a lot of light and was spacious enough for a work table and several art easels, as well as space for supplies and a chair or two. Arthur wanted to surprise Gina with the idea, so her mom had to stall and suggest they start with the servants' quarters.

There were four rooms in total. Each room was big enough for a single bed, a dresser, chair, and armoire. Gina, her mom, and Trisha set about taking the curtains down. They then moved the furniture onto the landing, except for the armoire, which was too heavy. Mr. Locke and Arthur would move them. Once the rooms were swept and thoroughly washed, and the walls painted, then the ladies can have the furniture moved back in. Trisha carried the curtains downstairs for washing. Gina's idea was to combine two of the rooms and make an office for Arthur unless he has another space in mind for his office. Mrs. Locke told her husband that it seemed that both Gina and Arthur want to make a room over for the other. Mr. Locke said they could discuss their plans further when Jr. and Eloise arrive tomorrow. "It's too bad Eloise can only stay one week," stated Mrs. Locke, "but I understand she has a job to get back to. And Jr. can only stay the weekend."

"Is it lunchtime yet, mother?" asked Mr. Locke. "A person needs nourishment to carry out all the work that needs doing. And I am sure Gina and Trisha could use some lunch also, as well as you," he added. "I was just about to mention we stop for a bit of lunch myself," stated Mrs. Locke. "Maybe afterward we can sit in the conservatory and enjoy our tea and cakes."

CHAPTER 37

It was hard to believe that two weeks have passed by so quickly. The next day while Gina and Trisha were working in the garden, Arthur and Eloise arrived. Eloise will be staying for one week, and then she had to go back to London because she has a part-time job.

Since it is almost time for lunch, Gina and Trisha cleaned themselves up while Arthur brought his and Christine's luggage up to their rooms. Mrs. Locke had lunch ready in the conservatory. Today Trisha's brothers came with her and had been "helping" Mr. Locke clean out the small barn. Mr. Locke and Dorothy agreed that he would not give them any chore that would be serious if not performed well, given their age. As they came running in for lunch, Mrs. Locke looked up, and seeing Mr. Locke; she smiled contently. She remembered the times past when there were children at the manor and the pleasant noises they made while in play. They exchanged news over lunch, and after a short rest, Trisha's brothers joined Mr. Locke and Arthur while Christine joined Gina and Trisha in the garden. Mrs. Locke stayed in the kitchen to make a special dessert for dinner. They had invited Trisha and her brothers to stay for dinner, and then Arthur would drive them back home.

After Arthur drove Trisha and her brothers home, Mrs. Locke brought some tea and cakes for whoever was still hungry out to the conservatory. She and Mr. Locke wanted to discuss the news they heard about Henry. "Have you heard the news about Mr. Chestermere?" Mr. Locke asked Arthur. "No, I haven't, what happened?" he asked. "Mr. Chestermere and another man escaped from the Bethlehem Hospital yesterday afternoon while they were out on a day trip," added Mr. Locke. He then repeated what DS Dunes told him, that the police did not know where he was, and if he was with the other man named Harry, who escaped with him. The London police went to Cockernhoe and Rumforton and would have extra constables stationed at the two villages for an unforeseen length of time. The constables were especially observing the activities of Dorothy (Trisha's mother) in Cockernhoe since she had been visiting Henry, and in Rumforton, they are watching Helen, Harry's sister. There had been no unusual activity from either woman. Naturally, the police had spoken to both the women's neighbors, and there was nothing now happening to arouse suspicion.

Trisha told the Lockes that her mother seemed a bit nervous with the presence of a constable. She knew they are watching her because she had been visiting Mr. Chestermere. She also felt and saw how our neighbors' stare and whisper when she was out and about. Her mother's friend in Rumforton, who is Harry's sister, also felt the stress of having a constable hanging around. Both my mom and her friend's employers were very understanding, for which they were both grateful.

"All anyone can do is try to carry on as usual," responded Mr. Locke. "That is the advice DS Dunes gave us. We understand it won't be so easy for your mother and her friend, but if they don't know where the men are, then they should be beyond suspicion. DS Dunes had also suggested we get a dog, so maybe you young folks can drive to the dog pound in Luton tomorrow."

The next morning, Arthur, Christine, and Gina drove to Luton to check out the dog pound. They were hoping to find a mature dog, one that would respond to commands and could also be trained to guard the estate. After taking a few out to the get to know area of the pound, they all settled on a tan and white boxer. That breed was known to be protective of its owners, which meant the dog would be the right choice for those at the manor. The dog is three years old and had to be given up due to allergies. The owners kept the dog as long as they could, but when their son was born, they decided not to put their newborn through the suffering of allergies. The boxer's name was Buddy, and it was agreed they would keep that name so as not to confuse him when they took him home.

On their way back, they stopped at the local pet store for a bed, a leash, a collar, a few toys, and, most of all, dog food. "And we can't forget a box of treats," Gina piped up. I think Buddy will be much loved. Just look at his darling eyes." "We will have to do some training when we get back to the manor," stated Arthur. "Buddy will need to be walked around the manor grounds and shown his boundaries. We don't want him wandering off." "We had several dogs as I was growing up," mentioned Christine. "I could help with the training. It shouldn't take too long, the man at the pound said Boxers are quick learners." "I know mom and dad would just love him," added Gina. "More than once, I heard of the dogs they each had growing up."

CHAPTER 38

While everyone was busy at the manor, Henry and Harry were also busy settling into a new routine. They found a modest boarding house for a reasonable price. Next, they both procured jobs. Henry found work as a gardener's assistant at a local nursery, and Harry would be a manual laborer at the same nursery. They were both pleased with how things were shaping up. It had been quite a while since Harry did any manual labor, but he took to it like he had been doing it all along. Henry was in his glory, working with plants. The language barrier wasn't too much of a problem. There were a couple of other employees at the nursery who spoke some English. Henry and Harry could improve in their French, and the French employees could improve in their English speaking skills. Henry had noticed that several customers were English. That was one reason he wanted to settle in Calais. People were coming over from England to shop or spend a day. This way, he and Harry wouldn't stick out like sore thumbs.

After about six weeks, while having dinner one evening, Henry told Harry that this short time in France had put some meat on his bones. "Looks like physical labor is good for you; I've never seen you look so fit. Maybe that should be added as a form of therapy at the Bethlehem Royal Hospital. What do you think?" "I must admit, I do miss doing some hard work," added Harry. "And may I say the same for you. This sunshine feels wonderful."

CHAPTER 39

E loise was enjoying herself so much being at the manor and helping with the training of Buddy; that she didn't realize the next day would be the last day of her visit. She had never in her life spent any time at such a relaxing place. She had hardly ever been too far from London. Her family usually would rent a caravan for two weeks and travel around over the summer when the kids were young. Now, and with her parents' job situation, they only go for a long weekend. "I will surely miss all this," she told everyone at dinner. "I appreciate your invitation, Gina." "No problem," stated Gina. "I only wish you could stay longer. I'll call you in a few days to fill you in on all we've done." "Thanks, and thank you, Mr. & Mrs. Locke, for your hospitality." "You're very welcome," added Mrs. Locke. "Your help was much appreciated." "If you're ready to go, we can head back to London," stated Jr.

In the past six weeks, the garden had been flourishing. Mrs. Locke asked Dorothy for a list of individuals in the village who could use some fresh vegetables because there will be an abundance, and we want to donate to the needy. Gina had been so busy with the cleaning and gardening she didn't miss Jr. too muChapter He would come out every other weekend. And during Gina's last week home, Jr. would come and stay at the manor, then drive her back to London.

Everyone loved Buddy. Mr. Locke took them all around the estate with Buddy to acquaint him with the boundaries. They would need to do that each day for about a week, then evaluate Buddy to see if he would need more training. Mr. Locke then said he would start on a dog house for Buddy after dinner, and asked Arthur is he would help.

Later, Mr. Locke received a call from DS Dunes with an update of how the search for the fugitives was going. He still advised them not to let their guard down. When Mr. Locke told him that they had gotten a dog, DS Dunes was pleased. He then told Mr. Locke that he would be coming for a short visit on Saturday. Mrs. Locke overheard that and exclaimed, "how lovely, I will prepare a light tea."

Since Arthur and Gina both told the Lockes of their plans they had for each other, the Lockes advised them to discuss their ideas with each other. Gina asked Arthur what he thought about using one of the servants' rooms as an office for him. He responded, "what a smashing idea." Then he told Gina of his plans to use the nursery as a studio/office for her. She replied, "I love that idea." They decided to start on the renovations the next day. "There was no need to buy any supplies," added Arthur. "There was plenty of extra materials in the storage shed we could utilize, and for my office, it is just a matter of finding a desk and book cabinet. Mr. Locke did mention that there is some furniture up in the attic, so then we can take a look after dinner."

CHAPTER 40

D S Dunes arrived on Saturday at about half-past eleven a.m. He accepted Mrs. Locke's invitation to stay for a light tea. He told the Lockes that there had been no further information to add about Mr. Chestermere's escape and that of another man. "Can you tell us anything about this other man?" asked Mr. Locke. "Is he dangerous?" "I can only tell you what I know," added DS Dunes. "He is from Rumforton. His sister(Helen) still lives there with her children. She and an acquaintance of Mr. Chestermere's (Dorothy), who is from Cockernhoe, have been visiting both these men regularly," "Yes, we know about Dorothy," mentioned Mr. Locke. "Her daughter (Trisha) has been helping Mrs. Locke working in the garden. Trisha told us that her mother and Helen were feeling lots of stress because they visited the men in Bethlehem and that their neighbors were whispering about them and suspected them of knowing where the men were." "That's understandable," stated DS Dunes. "It's the guilt by association syndrome, but if the ladies honestly don't know where the men are, then they should try not to let anyone else's opinion affect them."

"But enough of that subject, I want to know how all your plans are shaping up," added DS Dunes. "Weren't there plans to enlarge the kitchen garden and build a chicken coop? And I see you got a dog. It looks menacing enough to scare away any stranger. Is it a rescue dog?" "Yes, he is," added Gina. "Arthur, Eloise, and I went over to Luton to the dog pound. Did you see his adorable eyes? Mr. Locke brought him and us around the estate to teach Buddy the boundaries of the estate. We wouldn't want him wandering off. He is such an intelligent dog."

"I saw some chickens wandering around. I guess you did get at least one coop made," stated DS Dunes. "We sure did," added Arthur. "Those chickens are free-range egg-laying hens. Now we need to build a coop for the meat birds, and soon we can sell eggs and chickens to the villagers."

Mrs. Locke told DS Dunes that Arthur would transform the old nursery into a studio for Gina, while Gina and her father transform one of the servants' rooms into an office for Arthur. We got a lot done, but there was still so much more to do."

Mr. Locke will renovate the greenhouse so we can plant some fruit trees." "The kids only have about five weeks before they go back to college," stated Mrs. Locke. "We plan to have everything done by then, and it would be up to Mr. Locke, myself, and Trisha to be in charge of the upkeep. The garden had been producing for a while now, so with the help of Trisha's mom, we had been able to supply some villagers with fresh produce."

"I must leave now," mentioned DS Dunes. "I will keep you informed, either with a phone call or one of the constables who are in Cockernhoe will stop by. Thanks again for the tea."

CHAPTER 41

On a day when her sons went to the manor with Trisha, Dorothy took the opportunity to visit Helen in Rumforton. "How are you doing?" she asked Helen. "You look a little stressed," "You would too if you had to pack for three for two weeks. I did mention that we're going to London to visit with my mother for two weeks, didn't I?" Helen asked. "Yes, I do remember, sorry, I have so much on my mind. When do you leave?" "Tomorrow, and it can't be too soon," added Helen. "I'm getting a bit tired of suspicious stares and wagging tongues. Even seeing a constable walking around is getting on my nerves. This visit is our usual summer break before school starts. Will you and your kids be going anywhere?"

"Oh yes, we will also be heading out to London to visit with my sister, but not for another two weeks. I couldn't arrange any earlier days off from work," added Dorothy. "Trisha didn't want to come with us, because she loves working at the manor, but since Gina is still home, Mrs. Locke told her she wouldn't be needed for now, that she should take the break and enjoy her remaining weeks of summer holidays." "Maybe by the time school starts, there would be less interest in our lives by our neighbors. I do hope the guys are alright. Did you get any letters from your pen-pal yet?" "No, nothing yet," stated Dorothy. "Me neither."

"How did your visit with the Constables go?" asked Dorothy. "I didn't feel they were accusing me in any way. They were very polite and concerned. And since then, whenever I pass them on the street, they are always courteous." Yes, I noticed that, also," stated Helen. "I didn't feel at all like they didn't believe me when I said I didn't know where Harry was. And I didn't. Just because Henry said they might go to Calais, doesn't mean that's where they are."

"Can I ask why you never mentioned your mother visiting Harry?" questioned Dorothy. "They always had a strained relationship, even as we were growing up. When Harry left to go live with our father when he was eighteen, he and mom didn't keep in touChapter When he got back from the Suez Canal war, he stayed with us for a while. Then he went back to London, and that's when the trouble started. Because of issues during the war, he ended up at Bethlehem Royal hospital, where he met Henry. They found they had the war in common." added Helen. "I must go. I have to finish packing." "Enjoy your holiday," called Dorothy. "I'll call you when I get back from my holidays."

CHAPTER 42

The next few weeks at the manor were busy. Mr. Locke and Arthur got a dog house made for Buddy. They also finished turning the nursery into a studio for Gina. Meanwhile, Gina and her mom put the final touches on the one room of the servants' quarters for Arthurs' office. They also converted the greenhouse so they could plant some fruit trees. Mr. Locke and Arthur went to Luton and bought a plum tree and an apple tree. They also bought raspberry, blueberry, and strawberry bushes. Mr. Locke announced to Arthur, "I can already taste the delicious pies Mrs. Locke would make, as well as the preserves." And the idea Gina had to give fruit and vegetables to those in need in the village was great. Mr. Locke admitted to Arthur that he and Mrs. Locke are proud of him and Gina.

In a few days, Arthur would go to London to pick up Christine for her two week's stay at the manor.

"How do you think Buddy's training is going?" Arthur asked Mr. Locke. "You would think he was born for this," stated Mr. Locke. "Mrs. Locke loves him. When Buddy was in the house, he defers to Mrs. Locke, but when he's outside, he defers to me."

CHAPTER 43

A rthur and Christine arrived at the manor in time for lunChapter Christine filled everyone in on her news. Her parents had a pleasant visit and planned to come over again at Christmas. Arthur's grandmother had insisted they stay at her house. She and Arthur's mother get along very well with Christine's parents. After lunch, Gina showed Christine around at all the changes that they had accomplished since arriving home for the summer break. She was impressed with how Arthur fixed up the old nursery as Gina's art studio and approved of how Gina and her mother completed the work on the greenhouse. Gina brought Christine out to the garden to pick some produce that she plans to bring to a couple of needy people in the village.

While they were walking to the village, Gina told Christine about DS Dunes' visit. At the village, Gina introduced Christine to Trisha and her brothers. Trisha told Gina that they would be leaving for London on the six o'clock bus. "Have a good holiday," announced Gina.

The next two weeks were a matter of short daily upkeeps of the garden, as well as taking Buddy for walks. Arthur took the opportunity to show Christine around the area, especially to Cockernhoe, where he had friends. Before they knew it, it was time for them to go back to London. Jr. arrived and would be staying for the last week of Gina's holiday. He and Gina would drive to

Luton so she can pick up some supplies for her new art studio. That way, everything would be there whenever she comes home for the school breaks. She would also bring some of the supplies with her to London so she can work on some of the ideas she had.

Over dinner on Jr.'s first day there, Mr. Locke brought up the subject of Mr. Chestermere. Jr. told them that DS Dunes had come to his office for an interview. He asked Jr., "Does Mr. Chestermere know about the Forfeiture Act?" The reason he asked confirmed DS Dunes' thoughts that maybe Mr. Chestermere would not show up at the manor if he knew he could never inherit it. But since DS Dunes has no idea if Mr. Chestermere knew or not, then there was still a chance that Mr. Chestermere may one day show up at the manor.

"Wasn't the lady who was visiting Mr. Chestermere from around here?" Jr. asked. "Yes, she was from Cockernhoe. Mr. Chestermere knew her when he lived there, but since he was ten years older than she is, they did not know each other very well. He had asked that she visit him because he wasn't receiving any visitors and wanted to talk to someone from his home town, so to speak," added Mr. Locke. "Did you know that her friend from Rumforton has a brother in Bethlehem Hospital also and that he and Mr. Chestermere became friends?" stated Mrs. Locke. "They also escaped together," she added. "I do hope the police find them."

CHAPTER 44

Across the Channel, Henry and Harry were enjoying their freedom. Over dinner one night, Henry commented on the fact that he felt so relaxed. He told Harry that he enjoyed working with plants again, and the other staff were friendly and understanding of his lack of FrenChapter "I feel the same," admitted Harry. "We can practice our French in the evenings when we have dinner at the local café. I also enjoy the work I'm doing. I like this place, I could live here forever, but I do miss Helen. What about you, do you miss Dorothy?" "I do," replied Henry. "I never thought I would, but she was a major part of my life this past six months. And yes, I also feel I could live here forever. Maybe one day the girls can come for a visit, what do you think?" "You said it," agreed Harry. "When do you think it would be alright to write to them?" "In time," answered Henry. "We must be patient. Have you noticed any gendarmes hanging around the nursery or the area? Maybe the British police haven't thought to contact the French police. Hopefully, they won't, but when they find the car we abandoned, they will consider that we came over the channel."

"Helen's kids will be back at school in a few days. She always takes them to London to visit their grandmother," stated Harry. "I guess Dorothy's kids will also be going back to school," said Henry. "She told me they would be going to London to visit family. I think we can write to them in about a month. We can find out how things are at home. Dorothy told me that she and Helen both have pen pals from Calais, so if the authorities question mail from France, they can say that it is only from their pen pals." "Yeah, knowing the people in Rumforton, gossip will spread about Helen receiving mail from France, and some people might think it is from me," added Harry. "That's the trouble with small villages. Everyone knows each other's business."

CHAPTER 45

Gina and Jr. will be driving back to London the next day. Mrs. Locke was making a special dinner for them. The night before, Mrs. Locke was telling her husband how much she enjoyed having Gina home and will miss her terribly. "Try not to be too teary on her last day," cautioned Mr. Locke. "You may even get her crying, which might make me cry. After all, this is her last year, and then you will have her twenty-four hours a day. Plus, she will come home most weekends and for Christmas break, and spring break. I must admit I will also miss her and all the others that were here. It comforts me to know that she has such good friends."

After a teary good-bye by almost everyone, Mr. & Mrs. Locke took Buddy for a walk. He had become quite attached to Gina and needed some loving. That night at dinner, Mr. & Mrs. Locke looked around the dinner table and sighed. "It will take some getting used to it just being the two of us," Mr. Locke stated. In a week, Trisha will be back from London and would continue coming to the manor on Saturdays to help with the garden, unless Mrs. Locke calls her to come one other evening.

Gina was enjoying the first few days back at college, and seeing the new student's confused expressions reminded her of her first days. Catching up with all her friends and getting accustomed to a new routine, Gina felt exhilarated. There was so much to talk about; the first week went by incredibly fast. The only disturbing thing was when Gina saw George in one of her classes. It looked like he was peering at her from behind one of his textbooks. Creepy. Gina decided not to say anything to Arthur at this time. So long as George doesn't "happen" to be near where she and her friends were. George thought he would be happy to see Gina, but watching her and listening to her talking to classmates, he wondered what he saw in her. He decided that he would try to stay away from her because he didn't want any trouble from Arthur or Jr... Besides, during registration, he was captivated by one of the new students. This girl was shy but sweet looking. George offered to help her when he saw her look of confusion. Her name is Melody. "It's a beautiful name," he told her.

At the end of their first week, Gina, Eloise, and Christine got together for a day of shopping and dinner. Eloise and Christine both thanked Gina again for inviting them to the manor. Gina brought them up on all the plans she and Arthur had, and how Buddy was doing. "It's like he was born for life at a manor," Gina told them. "I'm sure mom and dad will spoil him." "He has such beautiful big eyes," added Eloise. "How can you not want to spoil him?" "Our dogs at the farm are somewhat spoiled, but that doesn't take them away from their duties," stated Christine.

CHAPTER 46

After a month had passed, Henry told Harry that it would be okay now to write to Helen, and he would write to Dorothy. "We have to wait until they answer to find out how things are going back home. I haven't heard about any escapees on the French news, have you?" he asked Harry. "Not a single word, but remember, my French isn't that great," stated Harry. "Helen and Dorothy will be able to tell us all the news. I'll write my letter tonight." "Remember not to divulge too much information or be too specific about what you ask, just in case someone happens to get a hold of the letter. I'm not sure what Dorothy has told Trisha, but we need to be cautious. Has Helen told you if she has mentioned anything to her boys?" "No, not a thing," Harry replied.

It has been an anxious couple of weeks since Henry and Harry wrote home. They were both grinning like young schoolboys when they got their letters. Dorothy mentioned in her letter that all was quiet in Cockernhoe. She said again about Trisha working at the manor and the fact that the Lockes now have a dog. She hopes all was well there and asks when she might be able to visit. She closes her letter with good wishes, and that she would look forward to another one soon. Harry mentioned that Helen also said that things were quiet in Rumforton. The boys were back in school, and their visit to London was enjoyable. Helen closed her letter with good wishes and also asked when she might expect to be able to visit. Henry and Harry were both happy with the news.

Dorothy mentioned to Henry that Gina and Arthur had gone back to London for their second year of studies. Dorothy also said that she and Helen were talking and wondering if they could get their mothers to come and look after their children, then they could come over to Calais for a couple of days visit over the Christmas break. Helen asked that they let them know as soon as possible so they can make the necessary arrangements.

CHAPTER 47

The past few months have been hectic for Gina, Eloise, Christine, and Arthur. They now have mid-terms to study for; then, they would be home for Christmas break. Gina had not noticed George around much, so she assumed he had given up. Arthur did mention that he saw George with one of the new registrants, a red-head named Melody. "Now that's good news," added Gina.

Gina and Arthur had only been back to the manor on weekends a few times since classes began. They had wanted to attend some of the numerous activities that the college was hosting. Mr. and Mrs. Locke decided to come to London for Thanksgiving weekend. They stayed with Arthur's mother and grandmother. They brought Gina and Arthur up to date on how things are at the manor. They had a man from Cockernhoe come to stay at the estate to look after Buddy and to keep an eye on things. They didn't feel comfortable leaving the estate empty, and they didn't want to confuse Buddy while he was still getting acquainted with his new home. The Lockes also informed them that they hadn't heard anything more about Mr. Chestermere. Mrs. Locke told Gina that the garden was growing, and she arranged for Trisha to come and help. As far as Mrs. Locke was concerned, Christmas couldn't come too soon.

One day when Gina and Eloise were walking to the café for a well-deserved break from studying, they met George and Melody.

George introduced them to Melody and explained how he met her. Gina noticed that he couldn't take his eyes off Melody. She said to Eloise that she didn't feel a bit creeped out. She noticed that Melody was a shy girl, but seemed nice. "I don't think we will have any more instances with George peering at us from behind bushes or through the café windows," Gina told Eloise. "Thank goodness for that," replied Eloise. "We certainly don't need anything extra like that while studying for the mid-terms."

With mid-terms over, students are preparing for a well-deserved break. Jr. came over to drive Gina home and would stay at the manor until Boxing Day. He would then return to London and spend a few days with his parents. Arthur and Christine would visit with Arthur's mother and grandmother until Boxing Day, then go to the manor until after New Year's Day. Then they would head back to London.

Christmas at the manor was quiet. Mrs. Locke brought Gina up to date on clearing the garden and preparing it for spring. She mentioned how the fruit trees in the greenhouse are thriving. Mr. Locke brought Arthur around to show him that the estate grounds are ready for winter and what he had planned for spring. Even Buddy was eager to run around with Arthur and Gina like he was showing them his territory.

Gina and Arthur stated," we feel relaxed and ready to take on the next semester."

CHAPTER 48

Harry and Henry thought it was a great idea that Helen and Dorothy come over to Calais for a few days. With plans finalized with the ladies' mothers, Helen wrote to Harry and gave him their itinerary. Both the ladies were very excited about their trip. Neither of them had ever been over to France. Word got out in Rumforton and Cockernhoe about the trip. Many of their neighbors were envious of them. Some of their neighbors joked about getting themselves a pen-pal. It's not often that one of them can afford to go anywhere.

The visit went very well. Harry and Henry both commented on how good it was to see someone from home. On the day the ladies left, Harry was quiet. He later confessed to Henry that he didn't realize how much he missed Helen. Henry also admitted that he had gotten used to Dorothy's visits. Henry stated that maybe the ladies could come again in a few months. But we cannot risk going there, he said. We need to keep our ears open to any developments in the police searChapter Over the next few weeks, Henry noticed that Harry was back to his old self. Little did Henry know that Harry has been forming a plan on how he could go over for a quick visit to Rumforton. Henry did not want to admit wanting to see the manor again for one last time. While he was in the library at Bethlehem, he came upon a law book and read articles about a Forfeiture Law, realizing it applied to himself. He wondered why no one told him.

His lawyer should have. The items bothered him for a while; that's why he put Dorothy's name on his visitor list. Through her, he could picture the manor and all she talked about if he closed his eyes. He hadn't told Harry or Dorothy about what he read. He's just happy to be out of Bethlehem hospital

Right now, it looked like Harry was more upset about not being able to go home. What should he expect, Henry thought, after all, Harry did commit a crime and was in Bethlehem hospital for a reason. It could have been worse, and he could have been sentenced to a London prison. I think I should keep my eyes on him, Henry said to himself. He also realized that Harry hadn't been on any medications since they left Bethlehem and wondered if he should suggest that Harry see a doctor.

In the meantime, Henry decided that he would carry on working and wait for the next letter from Dorothy.

CHAPTER 49

With everyone back from Christmas break, the college was buzzing with excitement. Gina and all the other second-year students were putting their noses to the grindstone. The atmosphere rocked with their combined energy. The feeling was like do or die.

Gina's marks from mid-term were A's, as well as Arthur's, Eloise's, and Christine's. Gina and Jr.'s relationship took on a more permanent status. Jr. had given Gina a promise ring after they got back to the college. He had been so nervous on the drive to London that Gina thought something was wrong. She couldn't believe it. Every so often, she would gaze at her ring finger. The ring's design was two heart-shaped stones entwined, one a pink tourmaline, for October (Gina's birthday), and the other an Alexandrile, for June (Jrs' birthday). All her friends were excited for her. They knew how much she loved Jr., but Eloise and Christine also knew that an actual engagement was a long way off since Gina intended to work with Arthur at the manor to have it become self-sufficient and prosperous. When Arthur heard that they are only promised to each other, he felt relieved. He thought she got married, she would move to London.

Time seemed to be going by so fast, as it's now time to study for mid-terms and then back home for spring break. Gina hadn't called her mother to tell her about the ring; she wanted to see her face when she showed her the ring. Only three years ago, Gina never thought she would be where she was now. She had been trying to imagine herself as co-owner of the manor. She knew how hard her parents worked when the Beavingtons were there. She also realized that it won't be a walk in the park. As her parents told her, the improvements she and Arthur have implemented so far were the right decisions; and the ones for the future would be great. Just thinking about those responsibilities made Gina a little nervous.

CHAPTER 50

Over the past few weeks, Henry had noticed that Harry has been quiet during dinner and didn't want to go for a walk and coffee at the local café like they usually did. He asked Harry if he was feeling okay. "I'm fine," replied Harry. "I was thinking about Helen and home. Do you think we will ever be able to go back?" he asked Henry. "So far, there hasn't been any news here about us, and from what the ladies told us, they don't notice as many police around the villages," stated Henry. "We have to be more patient," "I'm tired of being patient," snapped Harry as he stormed off. Henry understood how Harry felt. He would like to go home, but he knew it would take time for the police to decide when to stop looking for them. They would have to rely on news from Dorothy and Helen. Henry understood why Harry is homesick. It would be Christmas soon, and since the lady's visit, Henry himself had been thinking of Christmases back home.

Ahh, the weekend, thought Henry, as he yawned and stretched. Since he didn't have to work today, he decided to linger in bed. He looked over at Harry's bed and noticed that Harry wasn't there. Hmm, I guess he got up early, thought Henry, as he prepared to wash. He didn't see a letter that had fallen on the floor next to the wash table. After washing, he decided to walk down towards the dock and enjoy a leisurely breakfast at a café he and Harry happened upon during one of their walks. While enjoying his after-breakfast coffee, a few acquaintances stopped by for a chat. By the time Henry got back to his apartment, it is well past noon. He figured Harry would have come back and was wondering where he was. Neither of the guys Henry talked to had seen Harry that morning. Considering the mood Harry had been in, Henry thought maybe he needed some time alone. The guys invited him to a game of bowls, but he decided to stop by the apartment first to see if Harry was there, then go over to the bowling area. It was as he was preparing to leave that he noticed the note on the floor. He sat on his bed to read it:

Dear Henry,

Sorry for the short notice, I just found out last night that Jacques will be going to his family's farm for this long weekend, and he has invited me. I know you will be working, but the boss gave Jacques and me Monday off because there won't be any deliveries on that day. Jacques and I will be back later Monday. Have a great weekend.

Harry.

CHAPTER 51

Harry caught the first ferry crossing to Dover. He then hitched a ride asking to be dropped off in the middle of nowhere because he didn't want anyone from Rumforton to identify him, even though he had not been home for five years. He had wondered if he would recognize the way to the crofter's cottage but was surprised when he found it with no problem. Once inside the cabin, he breathed a sigh of relief. There were no signs that anyone had been around there for a while. He had planned ahead and brought enough food to last the weekend.

Harry thought it would be a good idea to wait until dark before venturing into Rumforton. In the meantime, he decided to look around. He stayed close to the cottage in case someone was nearby. Time seemed to drag, so he thought he would wander close to the manor. It was only about a twenty-minute walk from Cockernhoe, and he only wanted to have a quick look around.

Wow, Harry exclaims! He didn't remember the manor being so huge. He could see that the grounds were well taken care of. Henry told him that there was a greenhouse in the back and several sheds that were for storage. From where he was, Harry could see where a large garden was. It was bare now, as it was the winter season. When he saw the dog, he decided it was time to leave. He carefully wandered back to the cottage, keeping near the tree line, so he could slip in if anyone was coming. As he arrived back at the cottage, it had started to rain. So he picked up a book he had found on one of the shelves and decided to pass the time reading. After a few hours, it had stopped raining. The sun had already gone down, but with the stars shining, Harry would have no trouble finding his way to Helen's house. He would time his arrival for when most people would had gone to bed. He didn't even consider the foolhardiness of his actions. And that was one of the reasons he found himself in the Bethlehem Royal Hospital. He does regret what happened to that boy, but it was an accident. The only reason he wasn't sentenced to prison was that he served during the Suez Crisis. It was determined that he suffered from Post Traumatic Stress, so the courts sentenced him to Bethlehem Royal Hospital for fifteen years. He had already served five years but feels he has come a long way with therapy and medication. He hasn't needed any medication since he left Bethlehem. He feels great, although sometimes he does become impatient for things to happen. That was why he lied to Henry and came over to Rumforton; he was feeling homesick.

Standing across the way from Helen's house, Harry saw that she has lights on, meaning she has not gone to bed yet. He saw that she was standing at her kitchen sink. He is suddenly feeling nervous. How would she react when he knocks on her door; will it frighten her? Will she call the police? Maybe he could find a phone box and call her first. Just at that moment, she looks up and waves. Next, she's at her front door, waving him in. "What in the world are you doing here?" she asked him. "How did you get here? Should you even be here?" "Let me sit down first before I answer all your questions," stated Harry. "I could use a cup of tea." "Sorry," responded Helen. "I am just so surprised to see you, come in, sit down. Would you like a snack with your tea?" "If you have anything, that would be great," replied Harry.

"Well," asked Helen. "Why are you here? Are you planning to stay?" "No," answered Harry. "I'm not staying; I'll take the ferry back Monday. I left Henry a note telling him I went with a co-worker to his family farm. It is a long weekend in Calais, and since I didn't have to work, I decided to come home. I was feeling homesick. Can you blame me? It's been five years since I've been home." "Did anyone see you?" asked Helen. "Where are you staying?" "I'm staying in the crofter's cottage, and no, no one saw me. I didn't even see a police constable patrolling," stated Harry. "There will be one patrolling at about 11:00 pm. They started that practice about one year ago. It's nothing to do with your escape," mentioned Helen.

"Thanks for the tea. I should go. Can I come tomorrow evening again?" asked Harry. "I will be leaving Monday on the noon ferry, but I have to hitch a ride to Dover first, so I want to leave here early Monday morning." "Yes, please stop by tomorrow," puts in Helen. "Be careful not to be seen, even though the constable won't be patrolling for another hour yet. Someone may notice a stranger lurking around and report it to the constable."

CHAPTER 52

L ife at college was carrying on. The students who are in the last year of a two-year course were sticking close to their books. Spring break exams would be upon them before they knew it, so there was an air of seriousness about them. Gina, Eloise, and Christine still met regularly for tea breaks. Gina's and Jr.'s relationship was on a different level since he gave her the promise ring. As far as Gina was concerned, things couldn't be better. In just over five months, she would be home, putting to use some of what she learned at college. She was also anxious to get her studio set up. But, it was sad that three people had to die for her to be in this position. She had it in her mind to paint of portrait of the Beavingtons and hang it above the inglenook fireplace in the smaller reception room in the manor.

Arthur was also anxious about the final five months of classes, but wondered how his relationship with Christine would survive when she went back to Scotland. Eloise had come up with an idea for them. The place she works in was hiring for the summer. Eloise brought Christine there just for a casual meet with her manager. The manager was giving Christine a few days to decide. Christine called her parents and asked if she would be allowed to stay in London and work at Jessica Kingsley Publishers, where Eloise worked. Her parents realized their daughter did not want to be too far away from

Arthur, so they gave her their blessing. Christine could not wait to tell Arthur.

During their regular Sunday lunch at Arthur's grandmothers, Christine took Arthur for a walk and told him the news. He was quite happy about it. Even though Arthur would be living at the manor, the drive to London is only an hour, so he can go for a day and visit with Christine as well as spending time with his mother and grandmother.

CHAPTER 53

After Harry left Helen's cottage, she quickly phoned Dorothy. "You wouldn't believe who was just here," she whispered into the phone so she wouldn't wake her kids. "Who?" asked Dorothy. "Harry," replied Helen. "He left a note for Henry telling him he went with a co-worker to his family's farm for the long weekend. He knew that Henry would not have wanted him to come here; it's too soon after the escape." "Where is he staying, and how long will he be here for?" questioned Dorothy. "He is at the crofter's cottage and will leave early Monday morning to hitch a ride to catch the noon ferry," replied Helen. "He startled me when I saw him standing under the trees across the street. He will come tomorrow night again at about the same time." "Why did he take the risk?" asked Dorothy. "He said that since he left Bethlehem Royal Hospital and was now enjoying his freedom in Calais, that he missed home. It had been five years since he had been here. I think it was a foolish thing to do and I'm sure Henry will have something to say about it. Do you think I should call him?" "Yes, I think you should call,' stated Dorothy. "Did Harry even tell Henry where he was going?" "He left Henry a note saying he had gone to one of his co-worker's family farm and that he would be back Monday," added Helen. "I can understand how Harry feels," mentioned Dorothy. "But, if he gets caught, they will send him back to Bethlehem and probably add to his sentence. The same would happen for Henry. Since they like

Calais, they should stay there for a long while. Sooner or later, the police won't be actively searching for them. They may never be able to come home."

"Are you going to call Henry tonight?" asked Dorothy. "No," added Helen. "It's rather late; I will call in the morning after the kids go to school and before I leave for work." "Good luck," added Dorothy. "Call me tomorrow to tell me what Henry says." "I will, goodnight," replied Helen.

After talking to Henry, Helen felt like she was a schoolgirl and tattled on someone. Henry told her not to mention to Harry that she called. He would wait, hoping Harry would mention his visit soon after he came home. Helen could tell that Henry was quite mad at Harry, but who can blame him. Neither of them wanted to go back to the Bethlehem Royal Hospital. Henry decided that he would wait a day or two and give Harry the chance to confess. He told Helen that he knew Harry had not gone to Jacques's family farm because Henry saw Jacques at the pub Friday evening. After hanging up with Helen, Henry cursed silently, calling Harry a dam fool.

CHAPTER 54

I t's spring break. Only Gina and Arthur would be going to the manor for the two weeks. Eloise had to work, and Christine would be training during those two weeks to prepare her for full-time hours in the summer.

After Gina unpacked, she went in search of her mother. She found her in the garden. It looked like some of the early seeds have already sprouted, she noticed. Her mom and Trisha had been busy. Gina didn't want to just blurt out about the ring, so she resorted to flapping her hand around, hoping her mom would notice the ring. When she saw her mom's eyes widen, she knew she had seen it. "It's a beautiful ring," pointed out her mom. "Did Jr give it to you for Christmas?" "He wanted to, but the jeweler was late in sizing it, so he gave it to me when I got back to campus," added Gina. "Do you love him?" asked her mom. "I do," sighed Gina. "I'm so happy for both of you," she told Gina as she hugged her. "Let's find your father; he and Arthur will be finishing the chicken coop. I know he'll be surprised and happy," stated her mom. After more hugs and celebratory comments, Mr. Locke said, "This calls for a celebration. Didn't you make Gina's favorite cake for dessert tonight?" he asked Mrs. Locke. "Why wait, let's dig into it now while we enjoy a cup of tea," he added.

"What is the news of Christine and Eloise?" asked Mrs. Locke, "Christine will be training for her new job during the break, so she can only come here on the weekend," stated Arthur. "I will drive to London Friday evening and bring her here. Then I can drive her back to London Sunday afternoon, where we will have dinner with mom and grandmother. I want to be back at the manor on Monday." "Eloise will also work during the break. At least this way, she can still see Mike, since he hasn't decided what he will be doing after graduation," added Gina.

"I'm curious to see how things are progressing in the greenhouse," commented Gina. "I want to help with the planting. Oh, and will Trisha be coming over in the next few days?" questioned Gina. "She won't be able to come very often," added Mrs. Locke. "Her mother wants to do a spring clean and would need her help."

Mr. Locke and Arthur walked into the kitchen, wiping the sweat off their faces. "Mother," asked Mr. Locke. "Is there any of your delicious lemonade available, we're terribly thirsty." "We just finished the one chicken coop, and before we drive to Luton, we need some refreshment," added Arthur. "And maybe one of your delicious scones to go with it." "Do either of you need anything from Luton?" asked Mr. Locke as he helped himself to a warm scone. "I'll have a quick check while you're eating," stated Mrs. Locke. With everyone satisfied with the tea and scones, it was time to get back to work. Mr. Locke and Arthur are on their way to Luton, while Gina went up to her studio to do more organizing before she took Buddy for a walk.

CHAPTER 55

When Harry got back home, Henry decided he wouldn't question him. He wanted to wait to see if Harry would tell the truth about where he had been.

"How was your visit to Jacques' parents' farm?" Henry asked. "Is it a big farm, and what do they plant?" "It's rather small. They plant what they need and also have a small vineyard," stated Harry. "Is Jacques the tall guy with the earring in his right ear?" asked Henry. "Yes, why do you ask?" demanded Harry. "Oh, no reason," stated Henry. "There is another guy who works part-time, whose name is Jacques. I wasn't sure which one you meant."

To change the subject, Harry asked. "How was your weekend?" "It was quite relaxing," stated Henry. "I met up with some of the regulars after dinner and enjoyed a couple of hours at the local bar. I asked about Jacques because there was a guy named Jacques, but I realize now that he wasn't the one you were with."

"Well, back to the grind tomorrow, so I will say goodnight," added Harry. "Pleasant dreams," stated Henry. "I think I will just go for a short walk before turning in myself." I wonder how long it will take before Harry confides in me, Henry thinks as he walks along the boulevard. I'll have to be patient. Meanwhile, Harry was wondering why Henry seemed so curious. Does he suspect something? I'll have to wait and see, he decided, before falling asleep.

At work the next day, Henry overheard Jacques asking Harry if he had a good weekend. And it was the Jacques who had an earring in his right ear whom Harry said he was with. What is Harry up to Henry wondered. Time will tell.

During dinner, Harry mentioned to Henry that he thought he would like to get an apartment for himself. "Why would you want your own place?" asked Henry. "Well, a man needs privacy once in a while, if you know what I mean?" answered Harry. "Do you remember Monique, who works at the convenience store? She and I have been sort of seeing each other, and I would like to invite her over. It wouldn't be fair to you if I always asked you to go out for a while. With me having an apartment, Monique and I could hang out whenever and for as long as we want. Also, Monique has a roommate, and we can't always ask her to go out so we can visit. What do you think?" "You know I wouldn't mind vacating once in a while, but I do see your point," added Henry. "When do you think you will move to the new apartment?" "Soon," replied Harry.

While Henry was on his usual evening walk, he had thoughts of Harry running through his mind. It seems like Harry has a secretive look in his eyes since he came back after the weekend. Could it be that he should see about getting some medications; after all, it has been about eight months since we came here, and he had been taking meds daily. It must have some effect on a person's body, to be taking meds daily, then abruptly not taking any. I must keep an eye on him, but that will prove difficult since he wants to move out. At least I will still see him at work, and we can get together for a wine or coffee some evenings.

A few days later, Harry informs Henry that he has found a small apartment just a few blocks away. He will be moving in at the end of the week. "That's great," comments Henry. "Is it furnished?" "Yes, it is, thank goodness, because I don't want to spend money on buying furniture. I will just need the basics, like bedding and towels, like we had to buy for this place," added Harry. "What's it like?" asked Henry. "Is it on the upper floor, and how big is it?" "It's on the second floor and is about the size of this one," added Harry. "I will invite you over for dinner in a few days. What do you say to that?" "I look forward to that," stated Henry. "Don't forget to write and give your new address and phone number to Helen," added Henry. "Right, I'm glad you reminded me, thanks," mentioned Harry. "How about we go out for a drink?" "I'm with you," stated Henry.

CHAPTER 56

A rthur left after breakfast to drive to London to pick up Christine, who would only stay the weekend. She brought the news of Eloise and Mike. "Mike was helping with deliveries at Eloise's place of work. The regular delivery guy hurt himself and could not lift too much. It was a coincidence that Mike was picking Eloise up, and seeing the guy struggle, he offered to help. Eloise's boss then offered the job to Mike to help with the deliveries," stated Christine." How was your job training going?" Gina asked Christine. "I'm enjoying it very much, the other staff are friendly and understanding," added Christine. "They make me feel so welcome, and I appreciate the fact that Eloise mentioned me to her boss. I also have time to search for jobs in my field. My parents said if I could find a job by the end of classes, then I could stay in London. Arthur's grandmother offered me to board at her home if I do find a job. I feel so blessed to have met such wonderful people."

When Arthur got back from London Monday, Mr. Locke wanted to finish the second chicken coop. This way, they buy the chicks and get them settled before Arthur had to go back to college.

Gina was surprised at how fast her two-week break went by. She and her mother had been very busy with the garden and the greenhouse. They were happy with the fruit trees that they had planted there. Even some of the vegetables that had been planted early in the season were producing.

After their trip to Luton to buy chicks, Mr. Locke and Arthur were busy settling the chicks in the coop. They set up a heat lamp as suggested since the chicks were still tiny and would need the warmth to survive. Gina and Mrs. Locke thought the chicks were so cute but realized some of those cute chicks would one day be their dinner. Mr. Locke would go back to Luton later in the week to pick up some older chicks; to be put in the coop that was built for the layers; this way, the family would be eating fresh eggs soon.

Spring break comes to an end, and its back to the books. Gina would try to get home every other weekend before she felt she should stay at college to study for the finals in three months. She was excited about keeping up with the progress of the garden and fruit trees. Arthur was most anxious about the chickens. They would keep up with the growth at the manor with phone calls.

CHAPTER 57

Harry felt relieved that Henry didn't carry on about the fact that he wanted his own apartment. He and Monique would indeed wish to have privacy, but also Harry didn't want Henry to be aware of his comings and goings, especially since Harry knew he would be going back to Rumforton again. He didn't realize how much he missed home and family, and he also wanted to get a good look at the manor. After hearing Henry talk about it all the time, the work he did there and that he was bequeathed the manor after the death of his half-sister, whom he murdered along with her husband and daughter. Henry told him that the Lockes were managing the manor, and he knows that they are decent people. Harry wondered if Henry would ever get to live in the manor if his sentence was for life. He thought that Henry was fooling himself and had hopes of possibly being released on good behavior.

Much to Harry's surprise, there was another long weekend coming up in a month. He decided that he would again go to Rumforton. When he called Helen to give her his new phone number, he told her that he would be coming for a visit in about a month. "Do you think that was a good idea?" questioned Helen. "It's my home, too," yelled Harry. "I miss it," "Have you mentioned it to Henry?" asked Helen. "Why do I have to tell him, he's not my keeper," shouted Harry. "I don't need anyone to tell me how to live," he yelled. "Don't yell at me," said Helen. "I care, after all, mom always told me to watch out for my little brother. When you do come over, please be careful. Let me know what day and I will bring some food over to the cottage. How long would you be here?" "I only have two days, the rest of my time off would be traveling back and forth, like last time. I will call you a few days before I leave here. Take care," answered Harry.

Helen decided to call Henry just to bring him up to date about what Harry had planned. She realized that Henry was not Harry's keeper, but they have been through a lot together, and Henry had told her he does feel responsible for Harry. He agreed to keep an eye on Harry, but wouldn't say that Helen called him.

CHAPTER 58

Now that the "children" have gone back to London, the manor was so quiet. Mr. Locke saw his wife wandering around, looking lost. "Are you looking for something, my dear?" he asked his wife. "No, no, I'm remembering what was happening here just a few days ago, it's so quiet, don't you think?" she stated. "Yes, but that's to be expected. They said they would be back in two weeks for the weekend, and Gina said she would be calling regularly," pointed out Mr. Locke. "I know, I know," sighed Mrs. Locke. "But it's never the same. I will get used to it in a day or so." "Great," commented Mr. Locke. "I must get out and feed those hungry chickens, come on Buddy, we have work to do. Buddy followed behind Mr. Locke like he was his shadow."

"Yes, I must get breakfast ready, then it's out to the garden for me," added Mrs. Locke. "I will call you when it's ready." "Won't Trisha be coming over today?" asked Mr. Locke. "Not for a couple of days," added Mrs. Locke. "Her mother needs her at home." "Trisha had been a great help since Gina had been away," stated Mrs. Locke. "I know for a fact that Gina was impressed with her work. Her mother reminded me of a neighbor we had when I was growing up. What do you think of her brother?" "He is a very hard worker and a quick learner. His mother should be proud of him. I noticed that he got along well with Arthur," stated Mr. Locke.

"I heard that DS Dunes' wife is expecting a child," stated Mrs. Locke. "That's great news," added Mr. Locke. "Did he say anything about the search for Mr. Chestermere and the fellow he escaped with?" "No, all he was allowed to tell me, was that it's an ongoing case, but since we were in a way involved, he did tell me that so far the trail had gone cold, and their office had put the case on the back burner, meaning it's not as serious as it was. But, he did say he would contact us if or when they were apprehended."

CHAPTER 59

Henry suggested that he and Harry act like tourists on the next long weekend and go scouting around the area. "Sorry, I can't," stated Harry. "Monique and I plan to go to Boulogne-sur-Mer for that weekend, and she wanted to show me around." "Enjoy yourselves," added Henry. "I want to hear all about it." "Will do," said Harry. "Do you have any plans yourself?" asked Harry. "As a matter of fact, I think I'll take the train to Dunkerque for the day. I've read about it in school and heard about it so often, and since I'm this close, I've decided it's time to visit that area." "Enjoy your trip," said Harry. "I'll see you Monday night." "And you also," added Henry.

When Harry went to catch the first ferry, he felt he was being watched. I'm becoming paranoid, he said to himself. There was no way Henry knows of my plans. After Harry got off the ferry, he managed to hitch a ride from an older couple who were returning from a week in Calais. They dropped him in an area close to where it would be a short walk to get to the cottage. At the cottage, he noticed that Helen had left a good supply of food. He made himself a cup of tea and a sandwich and then settled down to read a book he remembered to bring along. After a while, he felt like he needed to take a nap. This way, it will pass the time before dark when he can go into Rumforton to see Helen.

"Helen," whispered Harry. "Is it safe to come in?" "Yes, the kids are in bed, but still be quiet." "How are you?" Harry asked as he hugged Helen. "I'm just fine. How are you doing? You're looking like a picture of health. The French atmosphere certainly agrees with you." "It's also hard work," added Harry. "How about a cup of tea and maybe some dinner?" "Coming right up," stated Helen.

"It's good to see you," said Helen, as she gave Harry a hug. "Did you have any problems getting here? Did you see any constables?" "No," added Harry. "Everything went smoothly. I got a ride from a very nice couple once I got off the ferry. They visit Calais quite often, so they told me if I see them again, they would be happy to give me a ride. How are the kids?" "They're just fine. As usual, they are counting the days until summer. Now that they are older, they enjoy their visits to grandma in London. There is so much to see," stated Helen. "I know what you mean, I didn't like going to grandmas when I was younger, but then London took on a whole new look once I turned 10," stated Harry.

"Did you tell Henry that you were coming over here?" Helen asked. "Why would I," said Harry. "I told you he's not my keeper. I had enough rules to follow while I was in Bethlehem. So, please don't say anything to him," "How time flies," exclaimed Helen. "It's past eleven p.m., and the constables have already been on their rounds. It should be safe for you to go,"

CHAPTER 60

H enry left Calais early to catch the bus to Dunkerque. He wanted to spend as much time there as he could and still have time to catch the last bus back. Walking around the area, he found it interesting but also found it sad. So many died, and for what? Just because one country wanted more than what it had. It wanted to be the most powerful country. Was it worth it? No. And I'm no better, thought Henry. I murdered three people so I can be lord of the manor. I deserved the sentence I got. Knowing about the Forfeiture Law (that I cannot inherit because of what I did). I have accepted the fact that I can never go back to England. I find that I like living in France. I may stay in Calais so that I could get over to England if I ever feel homesick. I enjoy Dorothy's company and would like to go further in our friendship. I would need to get acquainted with her children, but first, I will invite her here for a weekend and tell her how I feel, and hopefully, she felt the same.

Deciding to stop at the neighborhood café for an evening coffee, Henry saw Harry and Monique and joined them. He inquired about their trip to Hazebrouck. Monique looked confused and was about to answer when Harry added that it was a quiet little place, and the inn they stayed at was quite rustic. Before Henry had a chance to ask anything else, Harry quickly mentioned that he was tired from their trip and that he and Monique should be leaving. "Goodnight, Henry," he added. "You can tell me about your trip to Dunkerque at another time." For the rest of that week, Henry sensed that Harry was avoiding him. He hadn't been to the café in the evenings where they usually had a glass of wine or a coffee at the end of their day. One night Henry saw Monique sitting with a few friends and asked her where Harry was. Monique stated that she wasn't sure but that this was her night out with friends. She told Henry that she had plans to have dinner at Harry's the next evening. Could she give him a message? "No need. It's not important. I'll catch up with him one of these nights. Enjoy your evening, ladies," replied Henry.

The next evening during dinner, Monique told Harry that she talked to Henry last evening, and he asked where he was. Before Monique had a chance to continue, Harry got angry. He yelled that Henry isn't his keeper and why won't he mind his own business. Monique had never seen him this angry, and it frightened her. She told him that he was scaring her, and please calm down. He then yelled at her to never tell him what to do. "Leave me alone," he screamed. "Just go,"

CHAPTER 61

Three more months of classes, then the students would be stepping into the real world. Some of them are worried about the job search. Gina felt grateful that she and Arthur already have a "job" to go to. Jointly running the manor would be their job and a school of sorts. They will be learning as they go. Arthur had Mr. Locke to teach him about maintaining the outdoors of the manor, and Gina had her mother. Gina and Arthur would then switch teachers, and Gina would learn from her father, and Arthur would learn from Mrs. Locke. Eloise would be working full-time at the publishers as an apprentice. Her certificate in journalism would be the stepping stone to more duties at the publishers. Christine and Mike have part-time positions at the same publishers. Both of them would also be looking for full-time work in their respective fields.

Aside from sticking to the books, both Gina and Arthur were concentrating on their relationships. Arthur was grateful that Christine had a summer job at the publishers where Eloise works. She would be able to come to the manor on days off. And Jr. planned to be at the manor each weekend. Arthur and Gina wanted to devote most of their time to the running of the manor. There would be a lot to do. The garden would be in full bloom, which means daily weeding and harvesting veggies for manor use and preparing boxes for those in the village who were in need. Arthur would be responsible for the upkeep of the manor grounds with help from Mr.

Locke. Tricia and her brothers would be helping over their summer holidays with the garden and chickens. Tricia would also be helping with the overall cleaning of the manor rooms. Gina would set aside some time each day to go up to her studio to draw or paint. But they had to get through the next three months.

CHAPTER 62

Harry was so angry with Henry that he went to his apartment to discuss what he felt was Henry's interference in his life. "Why do you think you have to know everything I do and everywhere I go?" Harry yelled at Henry as soon as he entered his apartment. "What do you mean?" asked Henry. "You questioned me about my weekend at Jacques family's place and then about mine and Monique's weekend trip to Boulogne-sur-Mer. Who made you my boss?" "First of all, I do not believe you went to Jacques's family place, because I saw Jacques at the café that Friday evening and secondly, I asked you how was Hazebrouck, you said it was a nice quiet place, but you didn't go there, you were to go to Boulogne-sur-Mer. Also, Monique didn't go with you even if you went at all. I saw Monique at her workplace. "So, where did you go on both those occasions?" "It's none of your damn business," yelled Harry. "Just leave me alone, or else!" "Are you threatening me?" asked Henry. "That's not a good idea." "There you go again, telling me what to do, just because you're the lord of a manor, you're not my lord, go to hell," Harry screamed as he stomped out of the apartment.

When Harry didn't show up for work on Monday, his boss asked Henry if he knew if Harry was sick. Henry told him that they no longer share an apartment. ; then offered to call Harry. When he didn't receive an answer, Henry went to Harry's on his lunch break.

There was no answer then either, so Henry thought he would stop by Monique's place of work. When Monique told Henry that she was no longer dating Harry, so, therefore, didn't know where he could be, this worried Henry. He went back to work to bring their boss up to date. Henry suggested that maybe Harry had gone out for a short while to purchase something to help him feel better. He stated that he would stop by Harry's on his way home from work.

Henry, however, did think that Harry might have gone back to Rumforton. If Helen didn't call this evening, he would call her. In the meantime, Henry would enjoy his evening as usual. He found that he felt at home here and would not want to change it for anything. But, with Harry's behavior over the past while, Henry grew more concerned. Harry would not be able to stay in England; it would only be a matter of time before he was found and re-arrested. It seemed to Henry that Harry was not thinking about that. It would be his loss. Also, Harry would probably tell the authorities where Henry was. Henry may have to go further into France but would wait and see what developed.

The next morning Harry was on the first ferry.

CHAPTER 63

At the manor, Mr. Locke heard a sound but dismissed it as being the wind. But then Buddy started barking. It could be that the wind unnerved him because they haven't had such a strong wind since Buddy came to live with them. Mr. Locke called Buddy, and together they walked around the house and checked that all windows and doors were locked.

The wind also woke Mrs. Locke; when she nudged Mr. Locke, she found he wasn't in bed, so she went looking for him. She knew he was probably checking on things downstairs. She slipped on her slippers and went downstairs. She found him in the kitchen with Buddy. He assured her that it was just the wind and that everything was locked and secured. But since they were awake, they might as well have a cup of tea. Mr. Locke reminded his wife that this was the first extremely windy day that they've had since Buddy became part of their family and that he needed comforting. Since the wind was still blowing hard, they decided to bring Buddy upstairs with them. Buddy growled again, but the Lockes put it down to the wind and didn't pay it any mind. Harry heard the growl and decided to leave before someone came to investigate.

CHAPTER 64

Henry called Helen quite late. She hadn't seen or heard anything from Harry, so they concluded that he wasn't in Rumforton. Helen promised to call Henry if she saw or heard from Harry. It left them both wondering where he could be. Since Henry didn't have Jacques's phone number, he decided to wait until he got to work the next day to ask him if he knew where Harry was. When Jacques said he hadn't seen or heard from Harry, Henry began to worry. He didn't want to let Helen know how worried he was. He also didn't mention how Harry's behavior had changed.

The next day after her children left for school, Helen took her bike and decided to ride over to the crofter's cottage. She also was worried. Deep down in her heart, she felt Harry was near, and he was. "What are you doing here?" she asked, out of breath from the bike ride. "Why didn't let me know that you were coming, I would have brought some supplies. How long are you staying? What about work?" "Will you please shut up," he snapped. "Did you bring any food?" "Yes, I made a sandwich so that I could have myself a picnic. But you're welcome to it," she replied. "So, why are you here?" "Please let me eat in peace, and I will answer your questions after if that's okay with you," he snarled. Helen patiently waited for Harry to finish. "Well, how long are you going to be here this time?" asked Helen. "Did you get some days off work? Why didn't

Henry come with you? Dorothy would have liked to see him." "You are so full of questions," stated Harry. "Yes, I did ask for some time off work, and I will be here for a couple more days. So, can you get some more food ready for me and I will pick it up when I come to your house this evening? And about Henry, we are not Siamese twins; I am capable of doing things on my own, you know. In case you haven't noticed, I am old enough to be out on my own. Have you ever been to that manor?" "Only once," answered Helen. "Dorothy brought the boys and me there one Sunday afternoon. It sure is an imposing building. The Lockes are very nice people. Arthur and Gina were still at school in London. We got a little tour, and Mr. Locke explained some of the changes they planned to make. What had Henry told you about it? And how does he expect to inherit if his sentence was for life? Do murderers get out early for good behavior?" "Actually, Henry hasn't said too much about it, but I know he misses it," replied Harry. "It's his home, and he deserves to be the lord of his manor. But I guess it could never happen since he escaped. If he is apprehended, I'm sure more time will be added to his sentence. And I suppose the same would go for me. But I don't intend to go back. After I leave here, I plan to go further into Europe." "Be sure to let me know when you decide where you're going to settle?" asked Helen.

After Harry left Helen's that night with the bundle of supplies she prepared for him, she called Henry. "Sorry it's so late, but I wanted to let you know the news," she stated. "Harry is at the cottage, and he looks terrible. Like he hasn't eaten or cleaned up in a few days. He came here unprepared, so I made up a bundle of supplies for him, even some of my husband's old clothes." "Did he say why he decided to come over?" asked Henry. "No, but he was in such a mood. He snapped at me and sounded so angry when I asked him if you knew he was here," answered Helen. "I am worried about him. Do you intend to come over?" "Yes, I will ask for a few days off tomorrow when I show up for work," replied Henry. "I should be there Friday evening. Can I come over to your house? I don't want Harry to know I'm here." "You would need to come around 11 pm because Harry always stops by after dark, and leaves by 10 pm, and then the constables do their rounds. They're usually done by 10:30. I will watch out for you about then." "Okay, great; I'll see you about 11 pm then," stated Henry.

That night when Harry got to Helen's, he still looked like he had had a bad day, so Helen decided not to ask how he's doing. After

Harry ate, Helen suggested that he should be leaving soon. "Why, are you trying to get rid of me?" he demanded. "No, it's just that the constables will be going on their rounds soon," stated Helen. "You don't want to risk getting caught, do you?" "Okay, okay, I'm going," announced Harry.

CHAPTER 65

After Harry left Helen's, he decided to take another walk towards the manor. Just to have a look, he told himself. He would prefer to see it during daylight hours, but that would be too risky. Now that he knew there was a dog, he won't get too close. Standing there, looking at the manor in the moonlight, he came to understand why Henry loved the place. It's so peaceful and majestic, it gives a person a feeling of being home. It's a shame that Henry felt he had to murder three people in order to become lord of the manor. He must not have been thinking of the consequences of his actions. He's a bit like me, act first, then think of the consequences. That's why I was in the Bethlehem Royal Hospital. I'm sure Henry regrets what he did, I know I do, but we can't erase the past.

Harry would like to see the inside of the manor. The description Henry gave him, spiked his interest and eagerness to have a look. He saw the light come on and heard Mr. Locke talking to Buddy to assure him it was okay, that it was probably only the wind. Harry made a hasty retreat and planned to return at a later date.

The next night Helen noticed that Harry looked a bit more composed. At least he had washed and changed clothes. "What did you do last night?" Helen asked. "I read for a while, thanks for the flashlight by the way, then I went for a walk," stated Harry. "I realized that I had gotten too close to the manor when I heard a dog barking. I made a hasty retreat." "Oh! I forgot to mention, Dorothy told me they got a dog. Mr. Locke told her a manor wasn't complete without a dog," added Helen. "It must be a guard dog."

"I know how to handle dogs," mentioned Harry. "Remember that German Shepherd Grandpa got? It didn't take much for me to make him my friend. How are the kids?" "They're really good. Mom was here after school and took them to London for the weekend," replied Helen. "I got to have the weekend for myself, for once. After you leave, I'm going to have a nice long soak in the bath." "Is mom still disappointed with me?" asked Harry. "You know, she never visited me once in all the years I was in Bethlehem, even though she lives in London. What kind of mother would abandon her son that way? If she loved me enough, she would have gotten over her anger about what I did. Had she said anything to you?" "No, I tried talking to her once, but she shut me down, so I never brought up your name again, sorry," answered Helen.

CHAPTER 66

H elen called Dorothy to let her know that Harry was at the crofter's cottage and that Henry would be coming over the next evening. He would be staying at her place since her kids have gone to London with their grandma. "Why doesn't Henry stay at the cottage with Harry?" questioned Dorothy. "Henry said he didn't want Harry to know he'll be here. He hasn't explained it all to me, but judging by the mood Harry's been in, it must be something serious," stated Helen. "We are both very worried about him." "Why don't you want come for tea Saturday?" "Yes, I would like that. It would be nice to see Henry again," added Dorothy.

Helen had supper ready when Harry came by. She didn't want him to stay any longer than he usually did. If necessary, she would play the "I'm not feeling well card," so he would leave by 10 pm. Henry would be coming by around 11 pm...

Since Helen was watching for Henry, she had the door open when he showed up. She told him Harry had left about 10 pm but had forgotten his parcel. She also mentioned that she had invited Dorothy for tea the next day. As they were chatting in the kitchen, Harry, who had come back for the parcel he had forgotten, came up to the window and saw Henry. Again, he's in my life, muttered Harry to himself. Will I ever be free of him? As he turned to leave, Helen happened to look out the window and saw him. Harry turned and ran off. When she mentioned it to Henry, he wanted to go after him, but Helen cautioned him to wait until the constables have finished their rounds. Harry would probably go back to the cottage, and if Henry waits, hopefully, Harry would have had time to cool off. It was close to midnight when Henry started for the cottage. By then, a storm had come up with strong winds, thunder, lightning, and sheets of rain. It was pretty intense. As Henry approached the cottage, he was soaked through and noticed Harry running off in the direction of the manor. Now, why would he want to go there at this time, Henry wondered. He called to him, but the thunder drowned out his voice. So he followed him. As he got closer to the manor, Henry noticed that there were no lights on. He remembered that the Lockes always left at least one downstairs light on. The power must be out, he thought to himself.

He saw Harry go around to the back, probably hoping to get in by the kitchen. With the noise of the thunder, no one would hear if any glass got broken, including Buddy. As Henry got around to the back, he noticed Harry disappearing through the kitchen door. As he crept in, there was a flash of lightning, which showed Harry grabbing a knife and going up the back staircase. Harry was yelling," This is Henry's manor, everyone must leave!" Henry followed him, trying to shush him. Then when Mr. Locke entered the kitchen, he saw someone disappear up the back stairs. He took hold of Buddy's collar to silence him so as not to alert whoever had come into the house. He hoped that Mrs. Locke would stay in the bedroom with the door locked.

Henry caught up with Harry and told him to quit shouting and put down that knife. They needed to leave, Henry told him. But Harry didn't pay him any attention. He had a far-off look in his eyes and was acting like a deranged person. Henry thought that Harry had gone mad. He tried to grab Harry's arm, but Harry pulled away from him and lost his footing, falling down the stairs. During the fall, he bumped his head, and with the knife in his hand, had stabbed himself in the stomach. Mr. Locke arrived at the bottom of the stairwell at that time. When he looked up, he thought he saw someone at the top of the stairs. He called "Who's there?" There was no answer.

Since Harry wasn't moving, so Mr. Locke checked his pulse; it was very weak, and when he saw the blood, he knew he needed to call for help. When he went to check if the phones were working, the lights came on at the same time he picked up the receiver. After calling an ambulance, he glanced up the stairs and noticed a shadow on the wall. Who could the other person be, he wondered. He called up, but no one answered. Maybe he imagined it. Buddy was staying close to his side.

Shortly, he heard sirens. He hurried to the front of the manor to let the attendants in as well as the police. The attendants couldn't revive Harry at the scene, so they transported him to the nearest hospital, which is in Luton, but by the time they had arrived at the hospital, Harry had passed away.

CHAPTER 67

As Henry was running through the forest, he heard the sirens. Since the sound was so far away, he realized that they must already be leaving the manor.

The constables had contacted DS Dunes, who arrived within the hour. He must have pushed the speed limit, Mr. Locke, mentioned to Mrs. Locke afterward. After taking Mr. Locke's statement, DS Dunes went to Rumforton to tell Helen of Harry's accident and to take her statement. While talking to Helen, DS Dunes noticed what looked like a sort of relief come over her face. She told him that she did know he was going to escape but had no idea where they were going. After a few days, Harry called her and told her they had stopped in Calais. She asked about Henry, but Harry got angry with her and told her that he had moved on, so never to mention his name again. DS Dunes asked about Dorothy, but Helen said Henry put her name on the visitation list, since he had no one else to name and that they knew each other when they were younger. Helen told DS Dunes that she and Dorothy would visit Bethlehem together, and Dorothy helped her with the plans Harry had for when they escaped and went to the crofter's cottage to pick up supplies she put together for them.

DS Dunes then went to Cockernhoe to speak to Dorothy. After he confirmed her statement with Helen's, he made a few inquiries in Calais. The Calais police confirmed that two Englishmen were working there, but seemed to have disappeared. After conferring with his superior, DS Dunes told Helen and Dorothy that the case is considered closed and that they would probably only face some charges for aiding and abetting criminals. DS Dunes promised he would ask the prosecutor to go easy on them, maybe just put them on probation or have them serve community service. He told them that since they admitted to it, and it was only their first offense, and neither had a criminal record.

The next day Mr. Locke called Arthur, who was at his grandmother's, to tell him the news. Gina, Jr., and Christine were also there. They said they would all attend the funeral, which was to be in Luton.

AFTERWORDS

Gina and Arthur are home from college and begin to manage the manor.

Christina finds a full-time job in London and becomes a regular visitor to the manor.

Gina and Jr.'s relationship moves on to the next step.

Mike goes back to the United States after receiving a full-time job offer. Eloise plans to visit soon.

Helen and Dorothy plan a holiday to Calais to visit with their pen pals.

Henry is traveling through France.

Printed in the United States
By Bookmasters